A DOCTOR'S DILEMMA

LAURA SCOTT

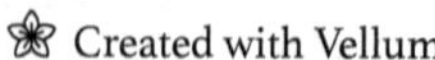 Created with Vellum

1

Flight nurse Kate Lawrence swallowed a laugh as she entered the hangar at Lifeline Air Rescue. She'd caught a glimpse of a funny sign on the side of a passing truck and wanted to remember the joke for her grandddad.

Katie girl, laughter is the best medicine. If people would learn to laugh more, you nurses would be out of a job. He was always trying to top her jokes, having passed along his quirky sense of humor to her. She needed to call him after work anyway, to make sure he was doing all right. Her parents were gone on their three-week European anniversary trip, and she promised to look after him.

She entered the debriefing room to find Lifeline pilot Reese Jarvis and Dr. Ethan Weber, the senior emergency medicine resident, on duty. Both already seated and apparently waiting for her. Was she late? She glanced at the clock to make sure she hadn't lost five minutes someplace. Nope, it was five minutes before seven. Whew. Reese grinned, but Ethan scowled.

"It's about time," Ethan snapped. "We've been waiting."

"Sorry." Even his bad mood wasn't enough to wipe the mirth from her face. The sign flashed in her mind again, making her grin.

"You think that's funny?"

"No, the sign I saw on the plumber's truck was funny. The slogan painted along the side of his van read: *Don't sleep with the drip, call me!*" She giggled. "I wonder how many women actually call him every day? Can you imagine?"

Reese chuckled, but Ethan seemed to have been born without the humor gene because he stared at her for a long moment as if she were some sort of alien species he needed to dissect and name. Finally, he looked away.

"Now that you're here, we can get started." He looked at the off-going shift doctor, Zane Taylor, and Ivan Ames, the paramedic on duty. "How did everything go last night? Any problems?"

The fact that Ethan didn't find the plumber slogan funny almost made her burst into another fit of giggles. Kate bit down hard on her lip to get herself under control. Humor was a good thing; she was a firm believer in the healing power of laughter. Her goal was to laugh every day, but clearly the handsome flight doctor didn't share her view. He wasted no time in getting down to business.

She remembered Ethan from the classroom training, but she hadn't flown with him before today. Since they'd just finished the final sessions a few days ago, it was possible this was one of his first solo flights. If so, maybe that explained why he was so uptight. Then again, he'd been seriously intense during the educational classes, too. And now that she thought about it, she couldn't remember ever seeing him so much as smile.

Hmm. Time to change that attitude.

"We responded to two flight calls during the night,"

Zane reported. "One was an ICU to ICU transfer. A nineteen-year-old male college student diagnosed with Wegener's disease was transported from Cedar Bluff Hospital to Trinity Medical Center with eight chest tubes, and—"

"Eight?" Ethan interrupted. "Not eight. You're kidding, right?"

Zane pursed his lips and slowly shook his head. "Not kidding. I counted. There were eight."

"Why on earth would anyone put in eight chest tubes? I've never heard of such a thing."

"I don't know, but I called the accepting physician to make sure he knew about them." Zane shrugged. "He did, so we took off. Luckily, the transport went off without a hitch."

"We'll need to do a post-flight follow-up visit," Ethan muttered. "Hope the poor kid makes it."

"He will." Kate spoke firmly because, along with humor, she also believed in positive thinking.

"Our second flight was a scene call, car versus tree," Zane continued. "Driver was intoxicated and suffered multiple injuries but should do all right. We transported him to Trinity Medical Center as well."

"Uh-oh. Score one for the tree, driver has a big goose egg," Kate joked with a wince. Medical humor could be a little on the grim side.

Ethan ignored her. "Weather conditions?"

Reese spoke up. "Temperature in the midforties Fahrenheit. Winds may be a problem—coming out of the north, gusting up to thirty miles per hour. No precipitation expected, though." Reese flashed a grin. "Hey, what can you expect from your average Wisconsin spring day?"

"Any pending flight calls?" Ethan wanted to know.

"Nope." Zane yawned widely. "You're in waiting mode. Anything else? I'd like to head home. I'm beat."

"Drive carefully." Ethan still didn't smile as he stood and slipped out of the debriefing room, heading for the lounge.

"What is up with him?" she wondered out loud, staring after him with a puzzled frown.

Reese shrugged. "He's new. I don't know much about him. Maybe he's nervous."

"Could be." She was willing to give the somber physician the benefit of the doubt. She didn't remember doing anything during training to merit such a standoffish response. Her gaze swung back to Reese. "Was Sam nervous during her first flight?"

"Yeah." Reese's eyes lit up at the mention of his new wife. The wedding had been small, but very romantic. Kate had shed a few tears when Dr. Samantha Kearn had become Dr. Samantha Jarvis. "She was but claimed my voice helped keep her calm and steady."

"I believe it." Kate had to admit, listening to Reese's husky voice in her headset was no hardship. Then she grinned. "Bet that trick won't work with Ethan."

Reese's eyes widened in horror. "I hope not."

Kate laughed and immediately felt better as she followed Ethan into the lounge. Obviously, she and Ethan had gotten off to a bad start, although she didn't know why. She shrugged. Since Ethan would be around for the next three months and would no doubt spend at least a few shifts as her flying partner, she figured she better make amends.

Her gaze instantly found him, standing next to the leather sofa rummaging in a large backpack. She noticed he was tall and wore his dark hair on the longish side, a dark lock hanging over his forehead as he bent to his task. His shoulders were broad, tapering to a narrow waist, overemphasized perhaps by his one-piece navy blue flight suit. The dark shadow of his beard should have been a turnoff, but on him, the disheveled look was very sexy. Her pulse kicked up a notch.

Whoa there, she pulled herself up short. She wasn't the type to fall for a great-looking face. Not that she didn't like men, she did. But over the years her relationships had developed the same, predictable pattern. They started as two people out to share a good time, never managing to progress into anything romantic. The men she went out with seemed to prefer remaining good friends, nothing more.

She really didn't mind. She knew better than anyone that life was precious, and she had made the choice long ago to be positively cheerful, regardless what spitballs life threw at her.

Another lesson learned from her granddad.

"So, what would you like to do while we are in the wait-for-a-call holding pattern?" Kate crossed the room to open the cabinet above the coffeemaker. "Since all the paperwork is up to date, we have a choice of a deck of cards . . ." She held them up for display. "Or Monopoly." She wrinkled her nose. "I'm terrible at Monopoly, and you're probably a pro, so I vote for the deck of cards. I play a mean game of gin rummy."

"I don't play games. I have things to do." Ethan pulled out a thick notebook and laptop computer. Sinking into the comfortable sofa, he set the notebook near his right hand and turned his attention to the computer screen.

Things? She raised a brow. What sorts of things? Was he studying for his boards already? *All work and no play makes Ethan a very dull boy.* She bit her tongue to avoid saying the cliché that immediately sprang to mind. Kate reluctantly set the deck of cards back in the cupboard, then glanced at Ethan. She'd bet her cherry red convertible that his bad attitude wasn't a result of nervousness. Either he'd taken an instant dislike to her or he simply didn't care enough one way or the other to make an effort to be polite. Whatever the reason, it gnawed at her to know Ethan didn't appreciate the true value of fun.

Fortunately for him, she was the right person to show him the error of his ways.

She watched him for a moment, debating the wisdom of poking her nose where it didn't belong. Not that common sense had ever stopped her before. Ethan's brows were pulled together in a deep frown as if what he read on the screen pained him. She sighed. Maybe he had problems. Hey, who didn't? But problems were much easier to face with a light heart than a heavy one. Dr. Ethan Weber would be a hard nut to crack, but she was up for the challenge.

He needed to be rescued from himself before he started having blood pressure problems or migraines—or something worse, like cancer. A guy in his dire, funless state required the full Kate Lawrence humor therapy treatment. Eventually, when he learned how to laugh at himself again, he'd thank her. They would part as friends when he graduated from his residency in June.

There was a little pang at the idea of letting him go, but actually, one of the reasons she tended to avoid dating the transient flight residents was because they always moved on. Oh, she wasn't averse to going out to simply have fun, and it had been a while since she'd found anyone who needed to be rescued as badly as Ethan did. She enjoyed helping people, and wasn't that the reason she became a nurse? And what was there to lose?

Certainly not her heart. Keeping things light was a way to make friends, not romantic boyfriends. And she wasn't looking for anything more. Besides, most guys she dated didn't seem interested in permanent relationships. Especially once she taught them how to relax and have fun. Once they'd moved on, they remained buddies and pals.

In her humble opinion, you could never have enough friends.

Kate idly strolled the length of the lounge, watching Ethan from the corner of her eye as he meticulously scanned the screen, then took careful notes in the notebook. Curious, she edged closer, trying to see what he was doing. It didn't look like work, at least not by her definition. The header at the top of the screen caught her eye. Good grief, was he actually scrolling through some sort of online dating site?

Perpetually cranky, thirty-something-year-old white male, seeking women of similar age for an emotionless relationship. No one looking for a good time need respond.

She giggled at her own joke. Ethan snapped his head around to glare at her. Whoops. Her eyes widened, and she took a guilty step back. Rule number one: don't poke fun at someone unless they have already learned to poke fun at themselves.

"What are you doing? Looking for a place to live?"

Maybe he wasn't on a dating site, maybe he was on one of those online listings that offered all kinds of services, including places to live. If she were honest, she could see how finding a new place to live might be considered work by some people. Although, for her, it would be an adventure. She would love a new place to live. Something nice, upscale, yet allowed cats, maybe with a big pool . . .

"No." He scowled and returned his attention to the screen. Kate's fingers itched to snatch it away so she could read what he was doing for herself.

"Maybe I can help," she offered, inching closer. "If you

tell me what you're looking for, I can help you find what you need."

"I don't need help." Ethan didn't even expend the energy to meet her gaze. "Other than for you to be quiet."

Oh, sure. Was he so clueless he couldn't figure out that holding her tongue was her most difficult personal challenge? For being a nearly graduated emergency medicine physician, he certainly wasn't very observant.

Good thing she wasn't interested in anything more than being a friend to help him lighten up or she might have to take his rebuff personally.

At that moment, the phone rang. Praying for a flight call, Kate pounced on it. "Lifeline Air Rescue, may I help you?"

"Can I talk to my daddy?"

The childish voice in her ear caught her off guard. "Your daddy?" She glanced at Ethan, who was already leveraging himself off the sofa, a dark scowl creasing his forehead under the lock of dark hair. He made his way toward her. "Ah, sure, sweetie, he's right here." She handed him the phone.

"Carly? What's wrong, honey?" Ethan dropped his tone and turned away.

Kate automatically took several steps backward, giving him the privacy he clearly desired.

For once, she was struck dumb. She never would have suspected the grim man had a child. A daughter named Carly. She hadn't even known he was married. Her gaze dropped to his left hand holding the receiver, noting the absence of a ring. Which didn't mean a thing, she told herself just as quickly. Lots of men didn't wear their wedding rings.

"Calm down, Carly. Crying isn't going to help. Where's Mrs. Vanderhoff? Put her on the phone." When Ethan put his hand up to massage his forehead, Kate couldn't help but feel a spurt of sympathy. "Mrs. Vanderhoff, what's wrong?" He listened intently for several seconds, then sighed. "Uh-huh. I see. I'm sorry about that. Yes, I understand, but you know very well I can't leave work in the middle of the shift. I'll be home by seven-thirty p.m. We can talk more then. Goodbye."

Kate remained silent for several long seconds after he hung up the phone. She knew she should pretend she hadn't overheard his every word, but that seemed foolish. Obviously, his daughter was in some sort of trouble. Who was Mrs. Vanderhoff? And inquiring minds wanted to know: Where was Mrs. Dr. Weber?

"Ethan, is your daughter all right?" Kate considered the possibility that he was looking through computer sites to find reliable childcare. Poor thing. Her heart softened. "Maybe I can help."

"She's fine." His tone was clipped. "And I already told you, I don't need your help."

"But—"

"Listen." He spun toward her, his dark eyes flashing with anger. "Stop trying so hard. Can't you see I'm not interested?"

Kate's jaw dropped. "I—wait a minute. I'm just trying to be nice. Don't you recognize friendship when you see it?" She struggled to remain calm, taking a slow deep breath. She knew he'd be difficult, so why the sudden urge to defend herself? His lashing out at her was more than likely related to his distress over his daughter. No reason to take it personally.

Ethan raised a brow. "Friendship? I don't need a friend. If you're not interested in me as a potential date, then you must be nosy. Do me a favor and leave me alone."

Kate ignored the pang of hurt and lifted her hands in mock surrender. Time to back off. "Okay, fine. Forget I asked."

Their pagers beeped in simultaneous chirps. Kate read the message out loud. "Two adult victims of a motorcycle crash." She barely glanced at Ethan as she swung toward the door. "Where's Reese?"

"Last I saw, he was in the debriefing room." Ethan beat her to the doorway, poking his head through the opening and calling out to the pilot. "Reese? Let's go."

The three of them headed out to the hangar where the Lifeline helicopter stood, ready and waiting. Reese jumped into the pilot's seat, gesturing for Kate and Ethan to board as he started the engines. Kate donned her helmet, then grabbed the clipboard and began initiating notes of the response. All this technology and they still hadn't figured out a way to get the flight notes computerized.

She tried to ignore Ethan as he sat beside her in the small confines of the helicopter, but her gaze was continuously drawn to him. *I'm not interested. I don't need a friend. Do me a favor and leave me alone.* His blunt comments shouldn't have lingered like an aching tooth, but they did.

He was different than most men she'd befriended in the past. She was more aware of him on a physical level, her nerve endings tingling just by sitting so close. Very strange. She'd need to work hard to ignore the sensation.

If they hadn't been in a helicopter, heading to the scene of the crash, she might've taken the opportunity to tell him how laughter had been proven to produce more immunoglobulin A and B in the body's bloodstream, those higher levels helping to prevent disease. To explain how humor had been used successfully by physicians in treating high blood pressure in a group of patients where half of them could stop taking their medication completely while the other half used much lower doses. There was even literature proving how using humor in cancer patients dropped their need for pain medication by half.

Reaffirming the facts surrounding the purpose of her mission helped her to relax. Ethan needed her, whether he realized it yet or not. Laughter was a savior, a simple way of turning your whole life around, even when things were bleak. Wasn't she living proof? She'd been through a terrible time, yet she had come out on the other side.

Ethan needed this, not just for himself but for his daughter. She couldn't help remembering how the hard planes in Ethan's normally stern expression had softened when he'd spoken to his little girl.

Kate firmed her resolve. Carly, like any other child in the world, needed smiles and laughter and fun, too.

2

—————

Ethan mentally counted slowly to ten, trying to ease the weight of his personal problems from his mind. His daughter was fine, even if Mrs. Vanderhoff wasn't. His little minx had put sugar in the salt container, messing with Mrs. Vanderhoff's eggs and endangering her health because, of course, she had diabetes. How the woman could've eaten almost all of the eggs without noticing the switch was beyond him, but that wasn't the point.

Why did Carly constantly get into trouble? Every day with the nanny was a new adventure, one he was very unprepared for. He wanted to bang his head against the wall in frustration. The one thing Carly really wanted, he couldn't give her.

He couldn't bring Carly's mother back from the dead.

So now, thanks to Mrs. Vanderhoff giving her two weeks' notice, they were stuck searching for nanny number five. The weight of responsibility lay heavily on his chest.

His gaze slid to Kate, who intently completed what she could of the flight report. Even with the clunky headgear on, he could see the golden hue of her skin, softened by the blond strands of hair escaping her helmet. He felt a twinge of guilt for the way he'd snapped at her. She hadn't deserved his anger, but then again, she didn't realize how much her simple presence was getting to him.

Maybe once, a gazillion years ago, he would've been very interested. Kate oozed a sensual appeal he secretly craved. She was happy and open and honest, representing everything he couldn't have. Her inner glow was so bright it hurt to look at her, much less get close, like a moth too stupid to know the light would burn. He had more problems than he knew how to handle, without adding a woman like Kate to the mix. Her constant cheerfulness was wearying. He secretly thought of her as Polly, short for Pollyanna.

But he probably shouldn't have been so blunt. She had seemed more than just a little interested in him, personally. But maybe he'd misunderstood. Hey, for all he knew, Kate was friendly to everyone, sharing her strange sense of humor with whoever would listen. An odd thing for a nurse working in trauma. He marveled at the contrast.

Frankly, he'd never met anyone quite like her.

"ETA five minutes," Reese's voice hummed through his headset.

"Roger." He risked another glance at Kate. She was staring out the window, her normally bright hazel eyes dull and serious. He inwardly groaned. Her bummed mood was his fault for losing his patience. Why was he constantly surrounded by things he couldn't have? Other people had lives outside work. Lives that didn't include reining in an unruly daughter.

He was immediately ashamed of his thoughts. He loved Carly more than life itself, even if he hadn't been home as much as he should have been while she was growing up.

She had had a tough year, adjusting to their new, seemingly empty household. How many other five-year-olds have watched their mother die? During Carly's infant and toddler years, he'd spent too many hours working. Now he and his daughter were strangers when she needed him the most. She needed him more every day. Maybe she was constantly misbehaving while he was away, but at night she often awoke crying from her dreams.

Her nightmares.

There was no point in wishing things could be different. He needed to find someone talented enough to firmly yet lovingly handle his scheming daughter.

No, he amended swiftly, what he really needed was the woman who could fill the void left by Carly's mother. He didn't want a wife, not after the way he lost his first one, but there was no question his daughter needed a mother.

He'd do anything for Carly, even marrying someone he didn't love. He wasn't in the market for love anyway. Love hurt too much. But he'd find some woman to marry if that was what was best for his daughter.

"Ready?"

Ethan glanced at Kate, who was looking at him oddly. He hadn't even realized they'd landed. "Yeah."

Before he could unfasten his safety belt, Kate jumped out, rounded the helicopter, opened the hatch, and pulled out the gurney. She snapped the empty stretcher to its full height with one smooth, impressive move. He jogged to catch up as they approached the scene.

"Over here." A firefighter motioned them over. "The female passenger is okay, just shaken up a bit and covered with road rash. At least she was wearing a helmet. The driver isn't so good, though."

Ethan instantly saw what he meant. The male driver

appeared to be a huge, overweight man in his early 40s, with a big bushy beard. He was wearing an Orange County Choppers T-shirt despite the cooler temps. Unfortunately, the T-shirt was soaked with blood from the gaping laceration in his scalp. Kate knelt beside him, clucking under her breath as she connected their patient to the portable monitoring equipment.

"Now you did it, big guy. Got your blood, dirt, and stones from the road matted in your beard. Gotta tell you, this was not a good idea."

For a moment, Ethan fought the insane urge to laugh. Kate was talking to the guy as if his worst problem was going to be soaking the blood and debris from his beard. Ethan grabbed a handful of gauze and began to bind the guy's oozing head wound. The laceration wouldn't be sutured until the patient was in the emergency department where they could clean it properly.

"Pulse brady at forty-five, BP barely hitting eighty systolic. He needs more fluid, and I only have one good line." Amazingly, Kate's voice didn't betray the barest hint of stress. Considering her quirky sense of humor, she was surprisingly cool under pressure.

"I'll start another IV on the side." Ethan tried to concentrate on the task at hand. Thankfully, the guy had ropes for veins, enabling him to start a second IV without a problem. The moment he had the catheter in place, Kate handed him the IV tubing.

He glanced up, caught off guard at her efficiency. "Thanks."

"No problem. Let's get him on the gurney."

"First put a C-collar on him. Does he have any other obvious signs of broken bones?" Ethan took the collar from her hands and helped slide the hard plastic into place.

"Yeah, I think he might have a femur fracture on the right, and his wrist looks messed up. Must've been the side they fell on. The woman's road rash is mostly on the right side too."

Ethan finished his assessment, then with the firefighters' help, managed to get the hefty patient placed on the gurney. Kate was much stronger than she looked.

"Ready to go?" He strapped the patient onto the gurney.

"Yes, sirree." Kate lifted the monitor onto the stretcher and slung the supply pack over her shoulder. They wheeled their patient toward the waiting helicopter.

The noise of the chopper kept them from conversing as they lifted the patient inside through the back hatch. Kate nimbly jumped in after him. Ethan averted his gaze from her lithe figure, nicely displayed in the navy blue flight suit, as he closed the hatch behind her, then rounded the chopper to climb into the side door.

Absolutely no point in longing for a pretty but impractical toy, especially one he couldn't afford.

Even five-year-old Carly knew better than that.

Ethan tried without much success to block out the sound of Kate's voice echoing through his headset.

"So, big guy, what happened? Did you lose control on your motorcycle, or did someone cut you off? Hope you weren't drinking, my friend, or you'll find yourself in a heap of trouble when you come to."

"Kate, will you please stop talking to him?" Ethan couldn't stand one second more. "He can't hear you, and if he can, for sure he can't answer you."

She fell silent for a moment, then grinned. "You're right. I need to focus on the positive side of things." She turned her attention back to the patient. "Come on, big guy. You need to wake up, or I might be tempted to shave your beard."

Did she have a strange beard fetish? Ethan shook his head. Never mind, there was no logic in her chatter, so why was he looking for some?

Without warning, their patient thrashed heavily against the belt Kate had loosened around his legs to free the IV tubing pinned beneath. Ethan laid a firm hand on the guy's shoulder since he was positioned at his head. But Kate, who was seated on the bench seat running alongside the patient, was no match for the biker's flailing limbs. She tried to reach down to grab his ankle, but at that exact moment, his non-injured leg kicked up and his knee slammed her shoulder with enough force to send her flying off the bench.

"Oomph," she groaned as she staggered back up to her seat. Holding a hand over her shoulder, she gave their patient an exasperated look. "Ouch. What did you do that for? I was kidding about shaving you."

"Are you all right?" Ethan leaned on the patient harder and reached over with his other hand to tighten the safety straps. He wanted to give her a hand but didn't dare let go.

"Fine, I guess." Kate quickly secured the strap over their patient's legs, before reaching up to rub her shoulder. "Boy, did he wake up fast. I can believe he heard me."

Ethan barely refrained from rolling his eyes. "I doubt he heard you. His pupils are unequal; he's got a head injury."

"You don't know these biker dudes." Kate jotted more notes on her clipboard. "They are fanatical about their beards, something I learned the hard way. During nursing school, I accidentally shaved a biker's beard because it was in the way of starting a central line. Never mind we saved his life, he roared with anger once he woke up to find his beard gone."

Ethan had to suppress another urge to laugh. He could just imagine her as an eager young nursing school student shaving some biker's beard. Then he frowned when he noticed her massaging her shoulder again. "Are you sure you're okay?"

"Just a little sore." She rotated her arm, wincing as she did so. "Uh-oh, there he goes again."

Their patient shifted on the gurney again. This time, though, they had him securely strapped so he couldn't hurt anyone. Ethan had seen many head injury cases, and this agitated phase was always the worst. Their patient snaked out his good arm from under the safety strap. Luckily, Ethan grabbed his hand just in time to prevent him from yanking out anything important.

"Get wrist restraints, the safety straps aren't enough to hold him. We can't lose this endotracheal tube. He could die."

Kate was already wrapping one cloth restraint around the patient's ankle and securing the other into the frame of the gurney. "He's not gonna like this," she predicted. "It may cause him to thrash even more."

"Too bad." Ethan was sweating from holding the guy down with one hand and keeping the breathing tube in place with the other.

"There, all set." Kate smiled again after she'd secured the patient's non-injured hand. "At least his vitals are stable. The fluids are keeping his blood pressure reasonable. Hopefully, he'll be okay. Could be worse."

Ethan scowled again. Yeah, Polly, things could be worse. Like he could let himself imagine what kind of fun he could have going out with pretty Kate Lawrence. That would be worse. A lot worse.

"ETA five minutes." Reese's voice in his headgear was a welcome diversion.

"Thank goodness," Ethan muttered.

Kate strapped herself in for the landing. He noted she was still favoring her left shoulder. Once they had their patient safely transferred, he'd make her fill out an accident report.

Reese lightly landed the chopper. Closest to the door, Ethan jumped out first. Kate followed, and they both rounded the helicopter to pull the gurney out of the back. In the middle of pulling the guy out, Kate's left arm gave out, and the gurney tilted dangerously to one side as she nearly buckled beneath the biker's weight.

Ethan used all his strength to hold the gurney steady until they managed to get their patient safely on the ground with the gurney at its full height.

"Sorry," she mouthed. The rotating blades of the helicopter created such a racket they couldn't communicate verbally.

Nodding to show he understood, Ethan tugged on the frame and wheeled the gurney away from the helicopter.

Inside the trauma elevators, he glanced at Kate as they both ditched their helmets. Her brow was damp with sweat, and there were tiny brackets of pain at the corners of her mouth. "Are you sure you're all right?"

"Fine." She avoided his gaze as they descended to the lower level, housing Trinity Medical Center's emergency department. She kept pace with him, helping to wheel the patient into the closest trauma bay.

She gave an updated condition report, and within minutes they had the patient transferred onto the emergency department equipment. On their way out toward the elevator, Ethan reached out to grasp her hand on the opposite side of her shoulder injury.

Huge mistake. Her hand radiated heat, and when his fingers closed around hers, she stumbled toward him, coming close. Way too close. He could see the light sprinkling of freckles across the bridge of her upturned nose. Her lushly curved mouth parted in surprise. Ridiculously, he noticed how her eyes had turned a deep emerald green before sanity returned with a rush.

"Get that shoulder of yours looked at!" His voice was louder than he intended. "You almost dropped him!"

"But I didn't." Her response was quick, but the flash of guilt in her gaze belied her words. She shrugged off his grip, the corners of her mouth dipping into a frown. "My shoulder is fine. Just dandy."

"No, it's not. You need to file an accident report, too."

"Why are you so crabby? He didn't kick you." She jabbed the elevator button, and the doors closed, locking them in.

He struggled to breathe something besides the lemony citrus scent clinging to her. He wasn't crabby. She hadn't even begun to see him crabby. Slowly, he counted to ten, a trick he learned in dealing with his daughter. Counting to ten helped him regain a measure of self-control.

Kate leaned toward him. He swallowed a surge of panic and forced himself not to step back. Her eyes weren't green anymore but a bright, mischievous blue. Distracted, he stared. Did her eyes always change color with her mood?

"Thanks for your kind concern, Dr. Weber, but you're not getting rid of me so easily." The words had to be pure bravado, but her wide smile sent a flash of desire punching straight to his gut, tipping him off-balance worse than anything else could have.

Self-control? What self-control? Who was he kidding? Around Kate, self-control was a complete illusion.

Katie tried to ignore the ache in her shoulder, but pain dogged her every step. Ethan shoved an accident report form under her nose when they returned to Lifeline, so she filled the stupid thing out. But then they'd argued over her ability to work the rest of her shift.

For someone who made a dedicated effort to remain cheerful, she was failing miserably.

Maybe Ethan was the type of guy who loved to argue, but she was not in the mood. He was still cranky, but at least this time he was preoccupied with the severity of her shoulder injury rather than simply being upset with her.

"I'm calling Jared," he threatened.

"Oh, come on," she scoffed. Dr. Jared O'Connor was the medical director for Lifeline and their boss. "It's Sunday. Do you really want to bother him at home? For what? Who's going work the rest of my shift? Not his wife, Shelly, especially since she's been so sick with her pregnancy. But if you want to pull Jared away from his family on a weekend, go for it."

Ethan picked up the phone, then slammed it down the moment she finished speaking. Kate couldn't help but grin. She figured her last line had done it. The throbbing wave of pain hit her hard, but she had a wince and resisted the urge to rub her shoulder. Ethan wouldn't hesitate to use her weakness against her.

What she needed was a good laugh, but she didn't think Ethan would cooperate by distracting her with jokes. Not his fault, really, and he didn't seem to know how to laugh.

The pain in her arm wasn't getting any better, so working really was a bit of a problem. Maybe they wouldn't get any more calls. A faint hope, but one she clung to anyway. Daytime on a Sunday could sometimes be quiet.

"Look, this isn't personal, but I need a flight partner who can lift patients." Ethan's voice was calm and rational. "I can't do this job myself."

Kate sighed, heading to admit Ethan was right. She glanced at her watch. There were at least five more hours until the end of their shift. "Who is scheduled for night shift? I can see if that person can come in a few hours early."

"And if they can't?"

"Gee, Weber, don't be such an optimist. Your cheerfulness is overwhelming." Kate tried to ignore his dour expression as she dialed Jessica's number.

Jess didn't answer, but Kate left her a message before hanging up. Ethan's scowl only served to make her feel worse. "You know, Reese would help with the lifting if we get another call."

"That's not in his job description," Ethan shot back.

Kate rolled her eyes at his negative attitude. She knew Reese Jarvis well enough to know the pilot possessed a strong sense of teamwork. "Trust me, Reese won't mind. Besides, what other options do we have? Until someone else can come in, you're stuck with me."

Ethan turned away, and Kate figured he felt as if being stuck with her was the worst thing he could imagine. She wished she could find a way to reach him. So far, she wasn't being very successful with her mission.

They didn't need to test Reese's willingness to lift because after an hour Jess returned Kate's call, agreeing to come in early to cover her shift. Kate tried to remain positive, to look on the bright side. Ethan would be better off having a flight partner who could lift. And this was the perfect time to step back and regroup. How was she supposed to teach him the value of laughter when she could barely dredge up a smile herself?

"You better go to Trinity's ED to have your shoulder looked at," Jessica advised when she arrived. "Remember how Ivan needed surgery after being slammed by a patient? You might need surgery, too."

"I'm so glad you brightened my day with that bit of happy news." Kate knew Ivan's surgery had been long ago, and his injury had been far worse. She preferred to think positively, but the pain in her shoulder was bad enough that she didn't dare ignore it much longer. Reluctantly, she took Jess's advice.

The ED was fairly busy, but they did send her for an X-ray to make sure there was nothing obviously broken. Finally, after a few hours, Dr. Hart, the orthopedic resident, returned.

"The good news is no broken bones. The bad news—a possible tear in your rotator cuff. We'll need to do an MRI to be sure."

Kate raised a brow. "Why do I need an MRI? How bad can a small tear be? I'm sure it will heal by itself in a few days."

"More likely a few weeks. Surgery is a possibility if it's a bad tear. I've got the MRI scheduled for eight o'clock on Tuesday morning. That's the earliest they could fit you in. But you better resign yourself to being off work for at least a few days."

To her dismay, Dr. Hart fit her with the shoulder sling. The idea of being off work while stuck with one arm in a sling didn't thrill her. At least Ethan would be relieved to know he wouldn't need to fly with her for a while. The idea made her sad. She'd failed in her resolve to teach Ethan to smile.

After gathering her prescriptions, she left the ED. Glancing at her watch, Kate realized it was seven thirty, just about the time she would normally be heading home. Steering the car with one hand was difficult, but she managed. With a grin and a light heart, she pressed harder on the gas and ignored her pain as she looked forward to spending some time with her granddad.

This break from work could be a blessing in disguise.

3

Granddad lived fifteen minutes outside Milwaukee's city limits. He owned a two-story house set in the middle of ten acres of wooded land. When she approached, Kate noticed a strange car parked in his driveway. Obviously, he had company.

Knowing her granddad, the visitor was most likely female. She didn't remember her grandmother very well; she had died when Kate had just been a young child. But over the years since, her granddad had kept a very active social life. A social life that included lots of women, usually a new one every couple of months. Granddad claimed he was just showing them a good time and couldn't settle down because he needed to spread himself around.

After all, Katie girl, single men my age are rare. I'm a catch, no doubt about it.

She and her granddad had always shared a special bond, ever since her rebellious teenage years. He'd pulled her through those dark days after her best friend had committed suicide. He'd taught her how to laugh at herself and to appreciate the funny things that happened in the world around them.

She could use a few laughs from him now.

Kate pressed on the brake, slowing to a stop behind the strange car. No doubt, Granddad was in his glory, telling jokes and sending his companion into fits of laughter. Did she really need to bother him by going in? Yes, she promised her parents to keep an eye on Granddad, so that's what she would do.

She climbed the steps to the front door, knocked, then waited. When no one came to the door, she pounded again, harder. Abruptly, the outside lights came on and her granddad opened the door.

"Katie girl!" His weathered face broke into a wide, welcoming smile. "What a nice surprise." He opened the door wider to let her in, then frowned when he noticed her shoulder sling. "What in blazes happened to your arm?"

"I . . . uh . . . hurt myself at work." She stepped inside and gave her granddad a hug with her good arm.

"Lifting patients?" He returned her hug with surprising strength.

"Not exactly, but I almost dropped one." Wryly, Kate remembered Ethan's horrified expression as they pulled the gurney out of the chopper only to nearly dump their biker patient on his head. Thankfully, Ethan's quick reflexes and amazing strength had prevented their patient from suffering a second head injury. Deciding Granddad didn't need to hear the details of how she'd obtained her injury, she changed the subject. "Is this a bad time? I noticed you have company."

"It's never a bad time for you, Katie girl." Granddad gestured toward the kitchen. "Come on, I'll introduce you to my friend, Miranda." He winked at her over his shoulder. "She's a younger woman," he said in a loud stage whisper.

Kate grinned. Since her granddad had just turned seventy-two a few months ago, finding a younger woman probably wasn't too difficult.

She followed Granddad inside. A trim petite woman with a cloud of pretty silver hair stood at the sink, washing dishes. The woman turned and smiled in greeting when they walked in.

"Miranda, this is my granddaughter, Kate. Kate, my friend Miranda Purdy."

"It's nice to meet you, Miranda." Kate offered a polite smile.

Miranda dried her hands on a towel and crossed the room to take Kate's hand warmly in hers. "It's nice to meet you, too. I've heard so much about you." Miranda sent her granddad an adoring smile. "I've been dying to meet everyone in Tony's family."

Kate raised a brow and glanced at Granddad in time to see a dark flash staining his cheeks. What was this? Her eyebrows rose higher. No snappy comeback? No jokes?

Belatedly, she realized there were candles on the table in an intimate place setting for two. Mentally, she smacked herself in the forehead. Duh. "I'm sorry. I'm interrupting your dinner."

"Oh no, don't be silly." Now was Miranda's turn to blush. The older woman, who is probably only in her midsixties, twisted her hands nervously. "We've finished eating, haven't we, Tony?"

"Yep, we sure have." Granddad's gaze softened when he looked at Miranda. "The food was excellent and so was the company."

Flustered, Kate took a quick step back. Oh boy, she was

intruding, big-time. Granddad's relationships in the past had all been lighthearted and fun. His attitude had been the more the merrier. But the atmosphere in the kitchen was decidedly romantic. A sparkle in Granddad's eye warned her that Miranda might not be like all the others.

Kate quickly backpedaled. "I can't stay, I have to get home. I only stopped in to see how you were feeling. Mom worries, you know."

"About me?" Granddad raised his hands innocently. "I'm fine, and you can tell your mother that if she calls. In fact, I haven't felt better in years." He winked at Miranda.

"Tony!" Miranda was blushing again. "You are such a tease."

Her granddad let out a hearty laugh, and Kate couldn't help but grin. True, his heart attack had been well over three years ago, so there really wasn't a need to be concerned. At the moment, he looked as healthy as he claimed.

Spending time with his new lady friend obviously agreed with him.

"It was nice meeting you, Miranda." Kate took another step toward the door. "I need to head home. I have to work tomorrow."

"Even with your sore shoulder?" Granddad asked.

Drat, she'd completely forgotten her shoulder. The idea of her granddad having a relationship with Miranda had blocked the pain right out of her mind. "Lucky for me, it's a work-related injury, which means they'll make me do paperwork or post-flight follow-up visits." She flashed a smile at Miranda. "I'm sure I'll see you again soon."

"I'm looking forward to meeting the rest of your family, too, Kate."

Granddad followed her outside. "Are you sure you're all

right, Katie girl? Is that shoulder of yours bothering you more than you've let on?"

"Not really." Although, all it took was to mention the pain for the feeling to return with a vengeance. "I'll be fine." She eyed the woman waiting for Granddad in the doorway. Should she ask about their relationship? No, better not. "Sorry for my lousy timing."

"Never too busy for you, Katie girl." His tone was casual, but she noticed he glanced back at the house as if anxious for her to leave.

She didn't need to be clubbed on the head with a brick, she got the point. After sliding into the driver seat, she started the car and slowly backed out of the driveway. Granddad waved as she left.

Kate drove home, trying not to read too much into the scene at her granddad's. Certainly, he deserved to live his own life. And if Miranda made him happy, great. Kate would be happy for him, too.

She just hoped Granddad wouldn't get hurt. He'd always claimed her grandmother had been the love of his life. Had something changed in the past couple of weeks? Why the sudden closeness with Miranda?

Later that night, sleep eluded her. To avoid ruminating on her granddad's love life, and the lack of her own, she focused her thoughts on Ethan and his young daughter Carly. From the little she's overheard of Ethan's conversation with his daughter, either he was divorced from his wife or his wife was out of town. Either way, he seemed to take everything about fatherhood very seriously. Maybe too seriously. Did he ever lighten up at home? Did he hunker down on the floor and play with his daughter? Did they swing on a swing set together, so high your feet almost touched the sky? Did he smile and laugh with her? Kate would like to think so, but the scenario was difficult to imagine.

Her eyes drifted closed. Her last conscious thought was to picture how handsome Ethan would look once he learned to laugh.

ETHAN DREADED TAKING his daughter to work, but what choice did he have? Carly was off school for the entire week due to spring break. Mrs. Vanderhoff didn't return for her scheduled shift, and though he'd called the nanny service several times, they weren't answering their phone this early. He didn't have many backup resources as his daughter's devious tricks had burned most of them out. He had no other option but to go to Lifeline and see if he could find someone willing to switch shifts with him at the last minute.

Outside, the fog hanging in the air lightened his spirits. They wouldn't be flying anywhere in this pea soup. It was barely 7:00 a.m., and Ethan felt as if he'd already put in a full day's work. Worrying about appropriate childcare was draining. And in the bright light of the morning, this idea of finding a mother for Carly, rather than another nanny, seemed ridiculous.

His wife, Susan, had been the perfect mother. One who had been content to stay at home and play with Carly all day. Susan had never once complained about how many hours he'd worked. How could he ever replace Susan in Carly's life? On the other hand, how would Carly benefit from a revolving door of nannies?

Things shouldn't be this hard, but no one had asked his opinion. For a moment, Kate's carefree, laughing face filled his mind. She'd use that Pollyanna skill of hers to find something positive in the mess of his life, he was sure.

"Good morning, Ethan." Jared O'Connor greeted him with a raised brow as he took in Carly's presence beside him. "I see you brought a visitor today."

"Sorry. Our nanny was a no-show." He grimaced. "I didn't know what else to do."

Jared waved off his concern. "Don't worry, she can sit here while we figure something out."

Ethan was grateful for his boss's supportive understanding. "Thanks. I'll make some phone calls straightaway."

"By the way, I heard you witnessed Kate's accident?"

"Yes. Our big biker patient kicked her right off the seat." Ethan frowned at Jared. "I had her fill out an accident report and sent her to the emergency department to get her shoulder checked out. Didn't she call you?"

"Not yet, but I'm sure she will." Jared rubbed his jaw thoughtfully. "I hope she didn't do any permanent damage."

"Me, too." Ethan glanced down at Carly who was tugging on his arm. He sighed. Patience wasn't his daughter's strong suit.

"Dad, can I play on the computer?"

He glanced at the computer screen in front of Reese, displaying current weather satellite readings. "No, honey, the computer is for work." He gestured to the computer, catching Reese's eye. "I noticed fog on the way in. How were the flying conditions?"

"Red for the moment. But the fog should burn off within the hour."

Ethan breathed a sigh of relief. He had an hour to find someone to switch shifts with him. He was reaching for the phone when Kate strode through the door.

"Good morning." Her sunny voice echoed off the walls,

and he nearly winced. What did she have to be so happy about? He tensed when her curious gaze zeroed in on his daughter like a homing pigeon. She immediately crossed the room with a wide smile. "Well, hello there. You must be Carly."

"Yeah. Who are you?" His daughter didn't have a shy bone in her body. Of course, neither did Kate Lawrence.

"I'm Kate, one of the flight nurses working with your dad here at Lifeline."

"Nice to meet you." Carly's polite tone surprised him. Ethan was secretly amazed his daughter could be so nice. Then she tugged on his hand again, and he tightened his grip in warning. "Dad, can I see the helicopter?"

"Not right now."

"Of course, you can."

He and Kate spoke simultaneously. Her lips twitched as if she were about to laugh, and her eyes widened innocently when he frowned.

"No, Carly, I need to make some phone calls to find someone to cover my shift." He worked hard to keep the edge from his tone, flashing Kate a look that clearly told her to back off.

"For today?" Kate's skeptical glance raked his flight suit. He was irritated with himself for noticing her expressive eyes were back to their normal hazel color. He should have figured Kate's nosy instincts wouldn't miss a thing. "What's wrong? Sitter problems?"

"Yes," he replied tersely. *Please, make her go away and leave me alone.* He did not want to answer twenty questions as to why he was having sitter problems. Carly was basically a good kid, just a little mixed up at the moment.

"I can watch Carly until you can make other arrangements."

"No, thanks." He knew his instinctive response was too quick by the flash of hurt in her eyes. Inwardly, he groaned. Why did he feel guilty? Kate was a flight nurse, not a babysitter. Besides, she thought his daughter was a sweet, polite little girl when he knew very well that Carly turned into a vixen the minute she was alone with a new sitter. Kate clearly didn't understand the circumstances surrounding Carly's mother. He knew he should explain the truth, but he didn't want to blab his personal problems for everyone to hear.

All he wanted was ten minutes of peace and quiet to make his phone calls. Was that too much to ask?

"Your choice." Kate avoided his gaze. "But I can't work your shift with the sling, and they'll need to cover my hours as well. Have you spoken to Shelly O'Connor? She has a friend who helps out with her son. Maybe her friend would be willing to watch Carly, too."

Ethan compressed his lips in a tight line. The idea was tempting, as long as Carly didn't try to annoy the other children, especially Shelly O'Connor's son. He knew the story of how Shelly's son was really Jared's nephew, but since her marriage to Jared, the boy was Jared's newly adopted son. His boss's son.

On second thought, juggling a shift with one of the other flight doctors sounded like a better plan. Or a safer one, anyway. He couldn't afford to lose his job. His luck, Carly would make Jared's son eat worms or something equally nasty. "First, I'll see if someone can switch with me." Stubborn, maybe, but he didn't care.

Carly tugged on his hand again. "Daddy, I want to see the helicopter! You said I could."

"I'll take her to see the helicopter while you make phone calls." Kate didn't exactly ask his permission but took his daughter's hand and led her off toward the hangar. For a moment he hesitated, then turned back to the phone with relief.

What harm could there be in allowing Kate to show Carly the helicopter? And he could use a few minutes to pore through the schedule, seeking someone who might be able to switch a shift with him.

He'd only completed two unsuccessful phone calls when there was a loud crash from the adjoining hangar. Immediately suspecting the worst, Ethan jumped to his feet and dashed through the doorway.

"Carly? What happened?" Wildly, he searched for a sign of his daughter's bright blond hair.

"I'm right here, Daddy." Carly stepped away from the aluminum rack located near a line of lockers, her angelic features exhibiting the familiar not-so-innocent expression. "I accidentally knocked over the helmets."

After reassuring himself that Carly was all right, he belatedly noticed several heavy helmets scattered over the concrete floor along with open spots on the aluminum rack where they were supposed to be. The grimace on Kate's features, along with the way she hopped awkwardly, favoring one foot, told him the rest of the story. His daughter had no doubt grabbed the helmets, causing them to fall to the floor, and one of them had hit Kate's foot. Good thing they wore steel-toed boots for flying.

Guilt settled like a heavy wooden yoke across his shoulders. Kate had already been injured once on the job. Did his daughter really have to make a bad situation worse?

"Kate, are you all right?"

"I'm sorry, Daddy." Carly must've sensed the tenuous hold he had on his temper because she hung her head, long blond pigtails falling forward to hide her face. She ran over to him, throwing her chubby arms around his legs. He reached down to give her a quick hug. No matter what tricks she pulled, he couldn't stay angry with her.

Losing a mother was hard.

"I'm fine." Kate forced a smile at his blatant expression of disbelief. Grudgingly, he had to give her credit for trying to maintain her Pollyanna attitude when she had every right to be angry. "Really. I think she scared me more than anything." Kate limped over to the helmet that had rolled the farthest and picked it up off the floor.

Yep, scaring people just happen to be one of his daughter's favorite pastimes. Maybe Carly had been simply curious about the helmets, but deep down he suspected she'd knocked them over on purpose.

"I'll take care of it." He released his daughter and crossed the room to take the helmet from Kate's hand. She stepped back as he collected the other helmets lying haphazardly on the floor.

Kate leaned down to pick one up, wincing as she did. "There must be a bright side to having a shoulder injury. I just need to find it."

What? A discouraged Polly? No way. He leaned down to lift the last helmet and carefully set it on the rack as he glanced at Kate over his shoulder.

"What did the orthopedic surgeon have to say?"

Kate smiled wryly. "Not much. I'm scheduled for an MRI tomorrow morning to rule out a rotator cuff tear. All from a little kick."

Ethan pushed the helmet rack up against the wall as a way to prevent Carly from accidentally hitting them again. "I have news for you. It wasn't a little kick. The guy weighed well over three hundred pounds and walloped you a good one." From the corner of his eye, he noticed Carly edging closer to the helicopter. "Don't even think about it," he threatened.

Carly stopped in her tracks, flashing a guilty look. He didn't have time to revel in his success for catching her before she did more damage because his pager suddenly shrilled loudly.

"I thought we were fogged in?" Ethan glanced at the pager. "Multiple motor vehicle crash involving a semitruck."

"Did you find someone to switch with you?" Kate asked.

"No." Grimly, he realized he'd been too busy chitchatting with Kate and cleaning up after his daughter to make additional phone calls.

Reese and Jenna, the paramedic on duty, entered the hangar. The pilot lifted a brow when he saw the three of them standing there. "The fog is pretty much burned off. We can respond to this call if you're willing to go."

Ethan swallowed hard, his mind whirling with possibilities, none of which he had time for.

Desperate, he turned toward Kate. "Can I take you up on your offer? Will you watch Carly for me?"

The flicker of hesitation in her gaze made his stomach clench with the sickening words. Had Carly's trick with the helmets given Kate second thoughts? He couldn't blame her if they had.

Then she smiled, and relief poured through him. "Of course, go ahead. I'll watch her."

Ethan nodded his thanks. Reese and Jenna were already opening the hangar door, preparing to pull the helicopter out for flight. He owed Kate big-time for bailing him out, especially after the helmet incident. No matter how difficult it was for him to talk about his wife, he needed to tell her at least part of the truth.

"Thanks. Carly has had a bit of a discipline problem since losing her mother to cancer last year. I'm not sure the helmets fell off the rack by accident. I'd appreciate it if you could stay here at Lifeline until we return from this call."

He braced himself for a burst of questions. Kate opened her mouth, then amazingly closed it again without uttering a word. She simply nodded as he plunked his helmet over his head, then dashed out to the waiting chopper, meeting up with Jenna and Reese.

As they lifted off, Ethan couldn't help but wonder how Kate would manage his unruly daughter. What an unlikely duo. Like ammonia and chlorine, Kate and Carly were at opposite ends of the chemical spectrum.

For some reason he couldn't quite define, he really wanted Carly to be on her best behavior with Kate.

Especially with Kate.

4

———————

Ethan tried to concentrate on the victim, but it wasn't easy. He kept thinking of Kate and wondering what devious tricks Carly was up to.

"Easy, now, just breathe nice and slow." He caught himself talking to his patient, the middle-aged semitruck driver, the way Kate would have if she had been there. Man, why did his mind always circle back to Kate? "You're going to be just fine."

Jenna the paramedic working alongside him, quickly strapped the trucker on the gurney. Ethan kept a wary eye on the heart monitor. Their patient was having the sort of EKG changes that led him to believe the guy had suffered a heart attack, either before, during, or after the crash. In these types of cases, there was a ninety-minute window of time that was critical to get the patient into the cardiac cath lab.

"Make sure those straps are tight," Ethan warned when their patient groaned. He didn't want to lose another partner to flailing limbs. "Then increase his nitroglycerin drip and give him another two milligrams of morphine."

"Got it." Jenna quickly did as asked, then slung their pack of supplies over her shoulder. "Let's roll."

Ethan nodded and helped push the gurney toward the chopper. They'd already been at the scene for twenty minutes, and again he found himself worrying about how Kate was faring with Carly. Normally, he thrived on scene calls, but not today. Reese couldn't fly them to Trinity Medical Center fast enough.

Between them, he and Jenna lifted the trucker into the back of the helicopter. Reese had the engine running, ready and waiting to take off. Ethan climbed in after Jenna and settled on the seat near the patient's head.

"His oxygen saturation has dropped to eighty-eight percent," Jenna noted.

"Increase his oxygen to six liters." Ethan didn't want to intubate the guy unless he had to. What was his name? If Kate were here, she'd know. He settled the headphones over his patient's ears so he could talk to him, then checked his wrist ID band, placed by the paramedics. "Larry. How is your chest pain?"

The patient groaned, shaking his head from side to side. Not good, apparently.

"Worse than before? Or the same?"

"Same." Larry's voice was faint through the intercom.

"Give him another two milligrams of morphine." Ethan was afraid the patient's heart attack was getting worse. He cued the mic so that only the crew could hear him. "Reese, I need to be patched through to the cath lab team. They'll need to meet us on the helipad for a hot unload."

"Roger." Reese sounded calm and in control. A minute later, Ethan heard a new voice through his headset.

"This is Dr. Arvani from the cardiac cath lab."

"We have an acute STEMI coming in from the field. I'd

like you to meet us at the helipad for a hot unload. We are thirty minutes in already. Reese, what's our ETA?"

"Five minutes," Reese responded.

"Sounds good," Arvani said. "I'll have a team waiting."

Ethan disconnected from the line, then double-checked the nitroglycerin drip. "Increase it again," he told Jenna. Larry seemed to be resting a little better between the nitro and the morphine, but his heart was still showing signs of heart damage.

"Got it." Jenna changed the rate on the IV pump and scribbled notes on the flight record. "Anything else?"

"Not right now." Ethan glanced at his watch. Four minutes to go before they'd land at Trinity. He felt good about having the cath lab team meeting them there.

Glancing down at Larry, he tried to reassure the guy. "You're going to be fine."

Larry didn't answer. Ethan knew if Kate were here, she'd be talking to Larry nonstop. Ethan wondered if her chatter would have helped Larry or made his chest pain worse. Either way, Ethan wouldn't have minded flying with her. Her serene demeanor and oddball sense of humor had a way of easing the tension from the situation.

Five minutes later, Reese landed on Trinity's helipad. He assisted Jenna in lifting Larry out and wheeling him toward the cath lab team. Together, they took the elevator down to the cardiac cath lab. Ethan filled Arvani in on the amount of morphine and nitroglycerin they'd given en route. The transfer didn't take long, but Ethan kept glancing at his watch. How long had Kate been keeping an eye on Carly? An hour? Surely, things were fine. Kate was an optimist, maybe Carly would respond to her positive outlook. How much damage could a five-year-old do in less than two hours?

Quite a bit if the helmet incident was anything to go by. Inwardly, he groaned.

Once Larry was undergoing his cardiac procedure and their paperwork was completed, they were free to go. Ethan tried not to rush Jenna, but he wanted to run with the empty gurney back up to the helicopter.

"I'm going to refuel before heading back," Reese told them, once he was seated in the back of the chopper with Jenna.

No! Ethan wanted to bang his head against the bulkhead. Refueling didn't take long, but in reality, every minute Kate was alone with his daughter was a potential disaster.

Somehow, he managed to stay calm until Reese landed the chopper at Lifeline. Ethan didn't care if he was the first one out of the chopper. He needed to know how Kate had fared with Carly.

When he walked through the door, his eyes widened in horror and his step faltered. Oh. Boy.

A bright pink gooey substance covered every surface, clinging to the lockers and the spare flight suits hanging nearby. The pink stuff was everywhere. The place was a total disaster, confirming his worst fears.

He swallowed hard. Where in the world were Kate and Carly?

Splat! He'd only taken a few steps when a gooey substance hit him square in the chest. Childish giggles reached his ears. He gasped. "What are you doing?"

"Carly, you can't hit your dad when he's unarmed," Kate protested. "Not fair."

His daughter continued to giggle, seemingly not in the least repentant. "It's only Silly String, Dad. Ooh, I got you, too, Kate."

Ethan peeled the neon pink strand away from his flight

suit, feeling the pressure in his chest tighten. This wasn't funny. This was awful. What had he been thinking, to leave the two of them alone? Not only was there a total neon pink mess, but Carly and Kate were both hopping on weird red and blue ball-like things with rubber handles, chasing each other around the hangar, shooting each other with the cans of Silly String. Kate was clearly losing the battle, hampered by her shoulder injury. His gaze narrowed when he noticed she held the can of Silly String with the hand in the sling, aiming at his daughter while hanging on to the ball with her non-injured hand.

What was she thinking? She shouldn't be using her injured arm at all, especially not for something as stupid is Silly String.

"Clean this place up, right now." Ethan used his deepest I'm-not-kidding tone. There wasn't a single surface untouched by the pink goo, leaving him no safe clean place to set his helmet. Annoyed, he tucked it under his arm.

Kate hopped across the room toward him, bobbing up and down on her ball as she eyed him curiously. "Lighten up, will you? We'll clean it up, don't worry."

Lighten up? Clearly her head was light enough for the both of them. Kate looked like she was enjoying herself a little too much. Right now, she could have passed for a teenager, bouncing on the rubber ball, with her long blond hair streaked with pink. He clenched his fingers into fists, why on earth did he have the insane urge to kiss her? "Does Jared know about this?" He pushed the ridiculous thought of kissing her aside. "And what on earth is that thing you're riding like a horse?"

"It's a Hippity Hop. Pretty cool, huh? I got the Hippity Hops and Silly String at the supermarket in town. Jared had to leave. I think he mentioned something about Shelly having a doctor appointment."

Figured Jared was gone. No wonder the place was trashed. If Jared had been there, Ethan was sure the Silly String war wouldn't have happened. At least, not to this extent.

"Hey, at least we managed to have fun, right, Carly?" Kate grinned.

"Right." Carly aimed a stream of Silly String at the back of Kate's head, then laughed when she scored a direct hit. Kate returned Carly's fire.

The mess faded as Ethan zeroed in on the sound of his daughter's laughter. When was the last time he'd heard his daughter sound so carefree? Months ago? Last year? Maybe Kate's methods were unorthodox, but despite everything, he could feel his mouth curving into a reluctant smile. "Maybe I should get myself one of those cans."

"Mine is empty." Carly's lower lip curled into a pout. "Kate, can I have some more?"

"Sorry, Carly, but I'm out, too." Kate raised her can and hit the sprayer to prove her point. Tiny puffs of pink goo fizzled from the can. "You know what this means, right? It's cleanup time."

Ethan steeled himself for the worst, knowing how much his daughter resented anything having to do with cleaning up, even if she was the one who'd made the mess. He eyed his watch with a sigh. Better to help Kate with the mess before making additional phone calls to find someone to switch for him.

"Okay." Carly stayed on her Hippity Hop but began to gather the remnants of Silly String. The pieces came apart in her hands and fell to the floor in small shreds. She glanced askance at Kate as if she'd done something wrong.

Kate frowned as she picked up a handful, too, a good portion of it falling to the floor in tiny pink bits. "It's supposed to be easy to clean up."

"And you believed that?" Ethan couldn't help his sharp tone, irritated all over again by Kate's naïveté. Where was her Pollyanna attitude now? "Get me a broom."

"Why would they lie?" Kate asked.

"Gee, maybe to make you buy the stuff?"

She ignored his sarcasm but abandoned her Hippity Hop and headed over to the small closet where the clean equipment was stored. Ethan suppressed a sigh. He supposed sweeping was a small price to pay for Carly's laughter.

"Daddy, Kate said I can keep the Hippity Hop. And she wants to give you hers, too."

There was no way on this green earth he was riding that thing, but he forced a smile. "Great. For now, though, why don't you put them in the other room? I need to sweep up this mess and bouncing on your Hippity Hop and flattening the bits of Silly String isn't going to help."

"All right." Carly hopped away, dragging Kate's Hippity Hop with her through the doorway before disappearing into the next room.

Turning back, he noticed Kate sweeping awkwardly, once again using her injured arm. His previous good mood faded as he stepped toward her. "What do you think you're doing? Are you trying to hurt yourself more? Give me that." He tried to snatch the broom from her grasp.

She hung on. "I can sweep. It's my mess."

Ethan felt like a two-year-old fighting over a toy. He ground his teeth and tightened his grip on the broom.

"She's my daughter, which makes this my mess." He was

close enough again to see the sprinkling of freckles on Kate's upturned nose.

"Carly is a great kid, Ethan." Kate's voice was soft as she relinquished the broom. "You're very lucky to have her."

Abruptly, his throat tightened, and his annoyance faded. He was momentarily at a loss for words. He cleared his throat. "I know."

She was staring at him again, only this time her eyes were a deep, intense green. For a moment they simply looked at each other, then he forced himself to take a step back. What on earth was wrong with him? She had just been trying to be polite.

"I'm sure the doctor didn't put your arm in a sling for no reason. He meant for you to rest the injury."

"It doesn't hurt as bad today." Kate watched him sweep for a minute, then crossed to the sink and grabbed a rag. With one hand she ran it under some water, then used the cloth to brush all the pink bits from the surfaces and onto the floor where he could sweep them up. "I'm hoping to come back to work soon."

He concentrated on sweeping the concrete floor, but her words echoed in his head, and an irrational excitement flickered along his nerves. Would she be back soon?

And if she was, would he be scheduled to fly with her again?

For a moment, he felt as young as Carly. Which was absolutely ridiculous. Kate was a nice girl, but he wasn't interested in anything more.

But regret burned deep at how he'd rebuffed her earlier offer of friendship.

"Whoa, what happened here?" Reese frowned as he entered the hangar with Jenna at his side.

Kate knew the inside of the hangar looked as if a giant neon pink Super Ball had exploded, but how many times did she have to explain? You'd think these guys never once in their whole lives ever played with Silly String.

"Nothing happened. We just had a little fun. No big major crime."

The corner of Reese's mouth kicked up in a grin. He'd been much more likely to smile since his recent marriage to Dr. Samantha Kearn. "A little fun? I'd hate to see what this place would look like if you really got going."

She stepped in a pile of pink goo, and it stuck to the bottom of her shoe when she lifted her foot. What was with this stuff anyway? It was supposed to harden into a foamlike substance, making it easy to clean up. *And you believed them?* Ethan's voice echoed in her mind. She reached down to peel the stuff off her shoe. Yeah, okay, maybe she had been a little naïve.

She and Ethan worked together for the next twenty minutes, getting most of the Silly String into the garbage. She suspected they'd find bits of the stuff for the next few months, but she couldn't regret her decision.

Carly had needed to do something fun. And in her opinion, the sound of Carly's laughter had been well worth it.

The phone rang, and Reese leaned over to answer it. "Just a minute. Kate?" He turned toward her. "Phone for you. It's Jared."

Puzzled, she crossed the room to take the phone from him. "Jared? What's wrong?"

"Shelly's obstetrician put her on bed rest because she's been spotting. I'm taking her home now. Since you're officially on light duty, I need you to help me with the schedule.

Shelly won't be able to fly, and with you out as well, I'm concerned we won't have enough backup."

"Of course, I'll work on the schedule. I'm having my MRI tomorrow morning, and I can talk to the orthopedic surgeon again. If they allow me to take off the sling, and if the pilots are willing to help with lifting, I should be able to work my scheduled shifts."

"I might have to take you up on that offer." Jared's voice sounded grim. "Even if I wanted to hire another nurse or paramedic, the training alone is ten to twelve weeks. Not exactly quick relief."

"Don't worry about a thing. Just take care of Shelly. I'll figure it out," Kate promised.

"Thanks."

Kate hung up the phone. She felt bad for Shelly. Her fellow flight nurse had been so happy to be pregnant. It didn't seem right that she was now suffering this complication.

"Something wrong?" Ethan halted his sweeping to lean on his broom. The man was determined to get rid of every speck of Silly String.

She nodded. "Shelly is spotting. Her doctor has put her on strict bed rest. Jared's taking her home and wants to stay with her, but he's worried about the schedule. With both me and Shelly off, we're going to need more help."

Ethan frowned. "My sitter situation is only making matters worse. I'll call the nanny service again. Maybe if I pay them extra, they'll find me a quick replacement."

A tiny voice in the back of her mind wanted to ask exactly why he was having trouble with the nanny service in the first place, but she held her tongue. She wasn't an expert on childcare by any means, and really, it was none of her business.

During the time he'd been off on his flight, she thought about the startling news he'd tossed at her. His wife, Carly's mother, had died of cancer. How awful for them. No wonder he was solemn and tense. She remembered how she felt after her best friend David had committed suicide.

Poor Ethan. He needed her now more than ever. Mourning was to be expected, but his daughter was proof he couldn't grieve forever. When Kate had given Carly her own Hippity Hop and a can of Silly String, sheer joy had brightened her face. Surely, Ethan knew Carly was too young to cling to grief the way an adult might.

Kate headed toward Jared's office to pick up the schedule from his desk. She sat in an empty computer terminal in the general office area, then accessed the Lifeline staff phone list. Shelly was scheduled for the next day, the same day she herself was scheduled for her MRI. Even if she did get the okay from the doctors to continue working, she couldn't manage the whole shift. Maybe someone would split it with her.

She only made a couple of phone calls before Ethan came up behind her about five minutes later. "How does it look?"

"Not good." When he leaned over her shoulder to peer at the schedule on the screen, she sucked in a quick breath. The warm male scent of him clouded her senses, catching her off guard. "I did find someone to work the first half of Shelly's shift tomorrow. I'm hoping that after my MRI I can fill in the rest."

"Zane Taylor is going to come in today to finish off my shift. The nanny service promised to have a replacement at my house first thing in the morning." He paused, and Kate knew if she turned her head, just the littlest bit, her mouth would be at the perfect angle to kiss him. "Guess we'll be flying together after all."

"I hope you don't mind. About the lifting, I mean." She wanted to kick herself for sounding breathless.

"No." His voice was deep and husky. "I don't mind."

Oh boy. Every nerve in her body tingled with awareness. More rotten timing. Ethan was supposed to be her project, not someone for her hormones to get in a tizzy over. Besides, they were hardly alone, here at Lifeline. Reese and Jenna were somewhere. Carly was, too. She frowned. "So, where's Carly?"

Ethan abruptly stood, glancing around. "I'm, uh, she was just here a few minutes ago. Wasn't she?"

A sick feeling clenched in her stomach. "I don't know. I haven't seen her since you told her to get the Hippity Hop out of the hangar and into the lounge."

"Oh, man."

"Don't worry. We'll find her. She can't be far away." Kate jumped to her feet. "Check the helicopter. I'll look around inside."

Ethan nodded as they both took off in different directions. Kate found the Hippity Hops in the lounge, but no sign of Carly. She checked in every office cubicle before making her way into the hangar.

"Carly, you know better than to climb into the helicopter." She was relieved when Ethan clearly found his daughter, although his harsh tone made her wince. "It's not a toy."

"Sorry, Daddy."

"Yeah, I know. But you're always saying sorry without making any effort to behave."

Kate hurried over. "How about if I set up a game on the

computer? She can play while I finish making calls to fill holes on the schedule."

"No need." Ethan's facial features appeared to be carved from granite. "As soon as Zane shows up, we're out of here."

"I understand." Ethan no doubt felt guilty about misplacing his daughter, even for a minute. She glanced at Carly who looked just as miserable. Being a single father couldn't be easy for Ethan. Was he still grieving for his wife? The thought bothered her more than she cared to admit. "I'm glad everything worked out."

"Worked out is stretching it, considering the mess Carly made inside the chopper." Ethan jerked his thumb over his shoulder. "She opened up supplies and tossed the wrappers everywhere. Reese and Jenna are putting everything back together now."

Kate shot a curious glance toward Carly. The girl's head was bent as if she found her feet fascinating. Her tangled hair had long since come down from her pigtails, the tresses still holding remnants of pink Silly String.

"I'm sure Carly didn't mean to make a mess." Kate couldn't help defending the girl. Couldn't Ethan see his daughter was seeking attention the only way she knew how? "I bet she was playing flight doctor, using the supplies to take care of a really sick patient."

Carly lifted her head just enough to flash Kate a grateful look.

Ethan's eyes narrowed suspiciously, but he didn't comment. Zane entered the hangar, drawing their gaze. "I'm here, Weber, you're free to go home."

"Thanks, Taylor. I owe you one." Ethan's tone held unmistakable relief.

"No, it's not a problem. I have no life." Zane grinned at

Ethan's daughter. "Hey, Carly. How are you? Are those your Hippity Hops I saw in the lounge on my way in?"

Ethan muttered something not very nice under his breath. "How did you know what those were? You don't have kids."

"Doesn't everyone know about Hippity Hops?" A puzzled frown wrinkled Zane's brow. At Ethan's disgusted snort, he shrugged. "Guess not."

"Thanks again, Zane. I'll see you tomorrow, Kate."

"Tomorrow, then. Bye, Carly. I had fun playing with you today." Kate smiled.

"Me, too. Bye, Kate." Carly's forlorn gaze clung to hers as Ethan took her by the hand and led her out, her bedraggled pigtails echoing her sad expression. Kate wanted to follow, to convince Ethan to lighten up a little, but she turned to her computer and to the task of filling the gaping holes in the schedule.

The image of the two of them, both so despondent and lonely, haunted her long after they'd left. Carly had experienced a little fun during their Silly String battle, but what about Ethan?

When was the last time the seriously intense Dr. Ethan Weber had done anything just for fun?

5

E than tugged a comb through Carly's wet, tangled hair, attempting without much success to remove the bits of Silly String matted in the silky tresses. *Kate. This is all her fault.* What strange compulsion had possessed her to buy the darn stuff?

"Ouch, Daddy, that hurts."

"I know, honey, I'm sorry." After a few moments, he wondered if he should give up and try again in the morning. Maybe combing the stuff out would be easier if her hair was dry. Too bad he hadn't thought about trying to brush the spongy foam from her hair before she'd had her nightly bath.

If all else failed, he could always take Carly for a haircut. He didn't necessarily want to cut her pretty golden hair short, but at least it would eventually grow back.

"It's okay." When he hesitated, Carly quickly denied her earlier complaint. "I don't mind. I had so much fun today, Daddy. Can we buy some Silly String the next time we go to the store?"

"I don't know," he hedged, secretly appalled at the

thought. "Remember how hard it was to clean up? Maybe there's some other toy we could try instead?"

"Okay." His daughter seemed mollified by his half-hearted promise. "But, remember, you promised we could ride the Hippity Hops before I go to bed."

See, this was the problem when you made rash promises as a bribe to get your five-year-old in the tub. "I remember. There isn't much time, so we better get them now."

"Okay." Carly eagerly scampered off. Ethan tossed the comb aside and stroked his hands over his face. Man, he was exhausted. Seemed like he had been tired for years. Susan had died just one year ago, but in some ways, it seemed like ten years had passed. When would their life get into some sort of routine? How long would nightmares plague Carly, keeping her up at night?

He heard her giggle as she hopped through the kitchen, barely clearing the doorway to the living room, pulling the second Hippity Hop so that it bounced behind her. He tried to take a stance against bringing them inside. They were really outside toys, but since night had already fallen and there wasn't enough room in their single-car garage, he'd caved into her desire to bring them into the house for one last ride before bed.

He knew Carly needed discipline, but deep down he was a softy when it came to making his daughter happy.

"Here you go, Daddy." She glowed, despite her damp, tangled hair, gazing at him expectantly from astride her Hippity Hop.

Thankfully, there was no one else around to see him. Ethan reluctantly straddled the rubber ball and grasped the handle. He felt foolish, bouncing up and down on the thing, but the glee in his daughter's face was worth every second of feeling ridiculous.

"Come on, Daddy, let's play follow the leader!" Carly took off through the living room, bumping into the chair and the sofa as she crossed the room. He tried to tag along after her but got stuck.

"I think we may have to wait until we can take these outside to play follow the leader," he told her.

"Push the sofa out of the way, Daddy, there's plenty of room." Her exasperated tone reminded him so much of Kate he lost his grip and almost fell off the ball.

"Unbelievable," he muttered under his breath, steadying himself. He did as Carly commanded and shoved the sofa aside the few inches necessary to allow him to hop through the opening.

Strangely enough, his reluctance to ride such a goofy toy faded after a few minutes. Carly's laugh was contagious, and he grinned when she led the way through the maze of their house, giggling at his difficulty in following her. Finally, the hour grew late, so he halted the two-person parade. "Okay, that's enough for now. It's bedtime, Carly."

Her tiny face crumpled. "Do I have to?"

Man, he wished there were a way to make this part of the day easier for her. She balked at going to bed because of the nightmares. If he could take the nightmares away from her and have them instead, he would. Helplessly, he nodded. "I'm sorry, but yes. You have to go to bed."

"I don't wanna." She sniffled but didn't quite break into tears. "I want to see Kate."

"Oh, honey." He looked at her helplessly. How could Kate have made such an impression on Carly after a couple of hours? Although, he could admit to being preoccupied with Kate after meeting her, too. "I'm sure we'll see her again, soon."

Carly reluctantly abandoned her Hippity Hop and

padded toward her bedroom. He followed, standing in the doorway as she painstakingly changed into her nightgown, then headed into the bathroom to brush her teeth. He knew she dragged out the nightly ritual as a stalling tactic, but he couldn't bring himself to scold her.

While he tucked her into bed, she clasped her arms around his neck so tight he thought she might never let go. "Daddy?" Her voice was muffled against his shirt. "Do you think Kate would be my best friend?"

His heart wept, tears welling in his throat. "I don't know, Carly. She might. Don't you have a best friend at school?"

She pulled back, then slowly shook her head. "Not like Kate."

He knew Carly had friends, hadn't he invited every single one of them over for her birthday party three months ago? That Saturday had been the longest day of his life, trying to rein in ten rambunctious girls. With an involuntary shudder, he tried to remember which ones Carly had seemed closest to. His mind went blank.

What sort of father was he that he didn't know which friends she liked the best?

And what made his daughter latch on to Kate? "I'm sure Kate would love to be your friend."

"Good." She pressed her tiny face against his neck. He held her close, wishing more than anything he could bring his daughter the peace she deserved. "I love you, Daddy. Good night."

"Good night, honey." He pressed a kiss to the top of her head, inhaling the sweet, innocent scent of baby shampoo. An overwhelming sense of protectiveness washed over him. "I love you, too. Very much. I'll be here if you need me."

"I know." Her words were drowsy, her eyelashes already fluttering closed.

As he eased off her bed, he hoped tonight would be the one where she'd sleep a little longer before waking from her nightmares. Ethan watched her sleep for a few minutes, then turned and walked into the hall, leaving Carly's bedroom door open a few inches so the bright hallway light could spill into her room.

Padding into the kitchen, he pulled a root beer out of the fridge and carried it into the living room. He intended to turn on the television as a diversion to unwind but ended up stretched out on the sofa, balancing the root beer on his stomach, enjoying the silence.

Unbidden, thoughts of Kate filled his head. The sound of her laughter, the warm glow of her skin, the way her pert nose looked sprinkled with freckles. The sensual, lemony scent of her skin when he'd almost kissed her. Gulping a quick mouthful of the root beer, he shoved the image away. He was only human. He'd been physically attracted to women before meeting Kate, but resisting temptation had always been easy.

Until now.

What made Kate so different from the other women who crossed his path? He tried but couldn't quite point to anything drastically unique, other than her perpetual cheerfulness and lilting laugh. And wasn't it strange how Carly, the kid who made every nanny's life miserable, seemingly had no problem listening to Kate?

Not only had Carly listened to Kate, she even wanted Kate to be her best friend. His chest ached at the loneliness lurking beneath her wistful tone. Was Carly missing her friends because they were on spring break from school? Maybe he needed to arrange some time together with one of her school friends for a sleepover. Although when he tried something similar in the past, Carly's nightmares had awoken both girls and nearly three hours had passed before they'd finally fallen back asleep.

Ethan grimaced. Inviting a school friend to stay overnight was one answer, but the idea of asking Kate to befriend his daughter lingered in his mind. She knew more than most of the others did about his personal life. After his wife's death, he switched from his surgical residency to the emergency medicine residency because the hours in the emergency department were regular shifts, making child-care arrangements a little easier.

Or rather, the childcare arrangements would be easier if he could find a nanny who would stick around for more than a few days at a time. The wry thought brought him back full circle. Carly needed someone dependable to count on. Someone who would make her laugh yet toe the line when it came to discipline.

Abruptly, he straightened. Maybe Carly had been right all along. Instead of seeking a mother to replace the one Carly had lost, why not provide his daughter a friend? A best friend? Someone like Kate?

Of course. Asking Kate to be Carly's friend was the perfect answer to his problem. With a rush of relief, he stood and carried his empty root beer bottle into the kitchen. The more he turned the plan over in his mind, the more he liked it. After locking all the doors and shutting off all the lights, he headed to bed.

He looked forward to seeing Kate the next day, and not solely because he needed to talk to her about befriending his daughter. No, he was selfish enough to admit that he had a secret desire to spend time with her, too.

KATE WASN'T CLAUSTROPHOBIC by nature, but lying on her back, buried in the long, narrow tube of the MRI machine, she slammed her eyelids shut against a flare of panic. *Pretend you're sleeping*, she whispered in her head. *You're taking a long nap. Don't even think about how close the tube is to your face when your eyes are open.*

She concentrated on breathing slow and easy as the machine loudly clanked and whirled around her. Why hadn't she specifically requested the open MRI? Because she wasn't claustrophobic, that's why. If there were ever a next time, which she really hoped there wouldn't be, she would request the open machine. Finally, after what seemed like forever, the noise stopped.

Opening her eyes, she looked into the smiling face of the MRI technician. "Okay, Ms. Lawrence, we're all finished here."

"Great." Thankfully, she sat up on the table, gently rotating her stiff shoulder. "When will I know the results?"

"Normally, the doctor reads the results at the end of the day." When Kate's face fell, the technician hastily added, "I'll call him for you, if you'd like."

"Yes, please." At times like this, it paid to be a nurse. She knew how the system was supposed to work. Normally, the radiologist, Dr. Brooks, would read the MRI results, then call Dr. Hart, the orthopedic resident who ordered the exam. But in her case, she figured she could convince them to stretch the rules. "I'd appreciate knowing the results as soon as possible. Will you ask Dr. Brooks to call me at Lifeline?"

"Sure." The tech poised his fingers over the keyboard of his computer. "Give me the number."

Kate rattled off Lifeline's main number, then left. She threaded her way through Trinity Medical Center's radiology department until she was outside. The sky overhead was a dark pewter gray, but the clouds didn't look bad enough to ground them. At least, she hoped not. But as she strode to her car, the winds were high, blowing strands of hair across her face. She peeled them away from her eyes, grateful for the warmth inside her car as she shut the door behind her.

Lifeline was located right across the street from Trinity, so she was early for her half of Shelly's shift. Kate figured Jared wouldn't mind if she did more paperwork, she'd only gotten through the first week of the schedule.

Inside, she found the Lifeline crew sprawled in the lounge. Ethan caught her gaze, and she entered the room. "Morning, Kate. You are early, aren't you?"

Shocked at the way he'd initiated a conversation, she simply nodded. "MRI didn't take as long as I thought."

Ethan's brow puckered. "Did you get the results?"

"Not yet."

Dirk, the pilot, nodded at her. "Hear you're the one who let loose with the Silly String."

With an inward groan, she nodded. "Yeah? So?"

Dirk raised his hand as if to ward off the retaliation. "So nothing. I heard it was a disaster and wish I could've seen the damage."

She rolled her eyes. "I didn't cause damage. We cleaned up the mess without ruining a thing. Right, Ethan?"

Ethan raised a brow. Then cleared his throat. "To be honest, I, uh, had trouble getting the stuff out of Carly's hair."

"Really?" She suppressed a flash of guilt, worrying her lower lip with her teeth. "The pink stuff brushed right out of my hair."

"I gave Carly a bath first, which made the spongy stuff sticky. Didn't work as well."

"Ugh." Kate ran her fingers through her straight hair, imagining the mess. Poor Carly. "I guess I should have warned you about that."

He shrugged. "I'll try to get the rest of it out later."

Kate wasn't sure what to make of Ethan's uncharacteristically laid-back attitude. Where was the tense, overly serious guy from yesterday? Was it possible he was already starting to mellow out? "I can help, if you like."

His eyes brightened. "Really? Carly would like that."

Shocked speechless again, she simply stared at him. She'd made the offer more out of guilt than believing he'd actually take her up on it. She did her best to hide her reaction. "Great." Time to change the subject. "Tell me, did you guys fly today?"

"First thing this morning, we did a hospital-to-hospital transfer," Ethan informed her. "Our patient was a liver transplant candidate being sent from Brownsville Hospital to Trinity Medical. No problems in flight, the patient was unstable, but we managed to arrive without an issue."

"Good." She should be glad Ethan seemed to be in a much better mood, but she found herself intensely curious about this new, loquacious side of him. If she didn't know any better, she'd think he'd already gotten the full blast of her humor therapy treatment and had changed for the better. But that was hardly the case as she hadn't even begun to roll out her plan.

What had happened since yesterday? Why was he suddenly being so nice to her? Friendly?

Because he wanted something more from her? Maybe on a personal level? A shiver of awareness clenched her stomach.

"Jared called, he won't be in again today. He asked if you

would keep working on the schedule until he gets back," Ethan added.

Kate nodded her agreement, ignoring the wayward direction of her thoughts. Her job was to show Ethan how to laugh, nothing more. "Did he mention how Shelly was doing?"

"He said Shelly is doing fine. Just that he needed to stay home to finalize some arrangements." Ethan shrugged. "I didn't ask specifics."

Understandable, since it really wasn't any of their business. Yet the Lifeline family was a small one, especially the regular, full-time employees. Residents, like Ethan, came and went, but she and Jared and Shelly had worked together for a while now.

The phone rang. Dirk picked it up as he was closest, then handed the receiver to her. "It's Dr. Brooks, looking for you. I'll be the pilot's room if a call comes in."

"Okay, thanks." She took the receiver as Dirk ambled out of the lounge. She was aware of Ethan's penetrating gaze as she spoke. "Hi, Dr. Brooks, thanks for getting back to me so quickly."

"I figured you'd want to know your results. You'll be happy to know there isn't a rotator cuff tear in your shoulder after all. I'll send a copy of this report to the orthopedic surgeon. It's Dr. Hart, right?"

"Yes, that's correct."

"Good. Just go ahead and follow up with him. I'm sure there is physical therapy of some sort to help with the pain."

Relief washed over her. No surgery! Zippity do-dah! "Great. I'll make a follow-up appointment with them soon. Thanks for letting me know."

"No problem."

Kate hung up the phone and instantly did a little happy dance. "Woo-hoo! No surgery!"

Ethan frowned, reverting back to his serious self. "Still, you shouldn't lift until you're cleared by the orthopod."

"I'll be careful." Kate deftly unhooked the shoulder sling and tossed it aside, savoring the freedom of movement despite the flash of pain. "Although, you know very well what they're going to say. Take it easy but use the shoulder normally and exercise the muscles regularly."

"There are specific shoulder strengthening exercises that a physical therapist can teach you to do," Ethan corrected swiftly. "I did a surgical rotation on ortho, so I know what can happen if you injure it again. I mean it. Stay away from lifting, Kate."

"Really? You were in the general surgery residency program?" She pondered this bit of surprising news. "What made you switch to emergency medicine?"

Ethan's expression became guarded, and he stood, shoving his hands deep into the pockets of his flight suit. "Oh, I don't know, I just didn't want to spend the next four years of my life in general surgery, then another two to three specializing before going into a private practice someplace."

"Really." She suspected there was more to the story that he wasn't telling her. "When did you switch? A year ago? After your wife died?"

His gaze narrowed, and his jaw clenched. "Yes, if you must know, the surgical residency program takes a lot of time. Too much time I can't afford to spend away from my family. Carly needs me."

"Ethan." Kate took a few steps and placed a comforting hand on his arm. "I understand, and I admire you for what you've done for Carly. Didn't I already mention I think she's a great kid?"

For a long moment, he remained stiff and unyielding, then the muscles of his forearm relaxed beneath her fingertips. Reluctantly, she let her hand drop from his arm.

"Yeah, you did. She likes you, too. In fact, she talked about you last night before going to bed."

"She did?" How sweet.

"Yeah, she wants you to be her friend." His voice dropped low and husky as if he were asking her out on a date rather than discussing his daughter's welfare. "She has friends in her classroom at school, but you made such an impression she wants you to be her best friend."

"Of course, I'll be her friend." Kate was touched by Carly's response to their Silly String fight from the day before. The little girl's carefree laughter had sounded wonderful. Could it be that Ethan's daughter didn't get enough fun at home? The idea troubled her. "You know, Ethan, laughing is good for the soul. There is actually scientific evidence proving the positive benefits of laughter on the body. I know you and Carly have gone through some very difficult times, but a little bit of laughter in both of your lives will go a long way."

She mentally braced for an argument, but he simply stared at her. "You could be right about Carly. I have to tell you, last night was the first night in months she didn't wake up in the middle of the night, crying from a nightmare."

"Oh, Ethan." Kate's heart squeezed in sympathy. "Nightmares are awful."

"So how about it?" His gaze held hers questioningly.

"How about what?"

"How about getting together on our next mutual day off? To find something fun to do with Carly?"

Her heart leapt with anticipation. Yet, she knew he hadn't intended to ask her out on a date. This was for Carly, his daughter. Quickly she recovered from her momentary flash of disappointment.

"That's a great idea. We can take Tyler, Jared and Shelly's son, with us. With Shelly on bed rest, I'm sure she'd appreciate a break. Now, where should we go?" She thought for a moment, then snapped her fingers. "I know, we'll take the kids to the indoor waterpark at Wisconsin Dells. They'll have a great time. You will, too," she added.

Bemused, Ethan shook his head. "I don't care about me, I just want Carly to have fun. I'll leave you in charge."

Ha! Little did he know, this was exactly what she'd hoped for. An entire day to show Ethan the value of fun. Obviously, they both cared about Carly, but Kate knew his daughter wasn't the only one she cared about. Ethan needed to lighten up, too. By the time she was finished with Ethan, he'd be a new man.

A smiling, laughing, happy one.

6

———

Kate didn't have a chance to pin Ethan down on an actual date for their indoor waterpark adventure because their pagers went off. "Cedar Bluff Hospital is requesting an ICU transfer, a thirty-six-year-old woman with stroke symptoms," Ethan said.

"A stroke at thirty-six?" Kate quickly followed Ethan out to the hangar with Dirk right behind them. "That can't be right. She's too young."

Ethan's expression was grim as they climbed aboard the chopper and donned their helmets. Kate did a quick survey of the interior supplies, including the flight bag, grateful to see every item was exactly where it belonged. She then pulled out her Lifeline clipboard and began to make preliminary notations as to the details of the flight.

Slanting Ethan a curious look, she found him staring pensively out the window as if she weren't there. Puzzled by his troubled expression, she waited until Dirk had them airborne, then flipped on her microphone.

"Ethan? Are you all right?"

"Fine." His tone was curt, and he didn't smile. His gaze

slid from hers, and he didn't elaborate further. She suspected he wasn't fine at all, but this wasn't the time to press the issue.

Kate pushed another button on her microphone, connecting them to the paramedic base. "Base, this is Lifeline. We're going to need the transferring physician at Cedar Bluff to call us with report on this patient's condition."

"Ten-four, we'll get back to you."

Kate left the connection open and glanced at her watch. The flight to Cedar Bluff Hospital wasn't too long, but she would feel better knowing a little more about what was going on with their patient. There had to be more to the story, some sort of significant past medical history or medications the patient was taking to have caused stroke symptoms at such a young age.

Her mind slid from concern for her patient to Ethan. His reaction nagged at her. Had his wife suffered from something similar? All Kate really knew was that his wife had died of cancer. Cancer wasn't the same as a stroke, although there were certain types of cancer, leukemia for example, that made a person more vulnerable to blood clots. And blood clots could cause a stroke.

Or maybe his wife had been about the same age of thirty-six when she had died. Either way, she suspected this flight wasn't going to be easy for him. She glanced over to where he was seated so stoically across from her, wishing she dared to ask.

"Lifeline, this is paramedic base. We have the transferring physician on the line. She'll give you report on the patient you're picking up. Go ahead, Dr. Gaines."

Ethan grabbed the second clipboard. They both listened and took notes as the physician began to provide the patient's recent history and brief hospital course.

"Charlene Perkins is a thirty-six-year-old female, recently diagnosed with leukemia. She stopped taking her enoxaparin at home and developed a deep vein thrombosis. After she arrived at the hospital, she showed signs of neurological changes. Suspecting a stroke, we immediately started her on tPA and called for transport to Trinity Medical Center."

"What other medications was she on?" Ethan asked.

Dr. Gaines rattled off several medications Kate recognized as chemotherapy drugs, although cancer was not her specialty. Ethan asked a few more questions, then disconnected the call.

They were quiet for several long moments until Dirk cued the intercom. "ETA approximately five minutes."

Kate set her clipboard aside, then gently took Ethan's from his hands. He didn't seem to notice. Within moments, they began their descent onto the helipad.

There was no more time to talk as they quickly disembarked from the chopper. Before she could get over to help him, he'd pulled the gurney out himself, leveraging it to its full upright position.

Kate slung the flight bag over her non-injured shoulder, but Ethan quickly took the bag from her and placed it on the gurney. Since Dirk kept the chopper engines running, they couldn't communicate until they pulled off their helmets and headed inside the hospital where it was much quieter.

They took the elevator down to the emergency department. When they entered, they could easily pick out their patient because she was the only one with a half dozen hospital personnel huddled around her bed.

Ethan took charge, his pensive thoughts during the

flight pushed aside to focus on the here and now. "Dr. Gaines? Any change in Charlene's condition?"

Katie busied herself with switching over the IV fluids to their own helicopter appropriate portable equipment, listening to the conversation as she did.

"Not really. The bolus dose of tPA has already infused. We just started the continuous infusion."

"Hmmm." Ethan didn't say anything more as they quickly transferred the patient from the ED bed to their gurney. Once that was done, he pulled out his penlight and checked Charlene's pupils as Kate finished reconnecting the monitoring equipment. "Her left pupil is still larger than the right, although they both react."

"Yes," Dr. Gaines agreed. "Before we started the tPA, her left pupil didn't react at all."

Ethan took the paperwork from Dr. Gaines, flipping through the information to find the lab values.

"What about her family?" Kate asked as she finished with the equipment setup.

"She has a husband and a young son. They're already on their way to Milwaukee," the ED nurse answered.

If not for the way the paperwork in Ethan's hands abruptly trembled, she wouldn't have noticed his startled reaction. But he quickly pulled himself together.

"All set?" He tucked the discharge paperwork beneath the gurney mattress.

"Yes, we're ready to roll," Kate said.

"Good." He nodded at Dr. Gaines, then pulled the foot of the gurney as Kate pushed from the head of the bed. Her shoulder protested the movement, but she ignored the pain. Clearly, her minor injury was nothing compared to what this patient was suffering.

She didn't think she winced at all, but Ethan suddenly

pulled on the gurney hard enough that she didn't have to do anything more than steer as they rolled out to where Dirk waited in the helicopter. When he saw them coming, Dirk jumped out and met them at the rear of the chopper.

Kate tried to motion him back, but he didn't pay any attention, quickly helping Ethan lift the patient into the back hatch before nimbly jumping back into the pilot seat. Kate wasn't required to do anything more than shut the hatch behind Ethan and their patient with her good arm, then climb in the side door.

Within moments, Dirk informed them they were ready to lift off. Kate carefully put the headphones over Charlene's ears, then rested a comforting hand on her arm as she spoke.

"Charlene, we have you safely tucked inside the Lifeline helicopter. You're on your way to Trinity Medical Center. I don't want you to worry about a thing. I promise you are in good hands. We'll only be in the air for about thirty minutes, maybe less." Kate took Charlene's left hand in hers. "If you can hear me, Charlene, squeeze my hand."

To her surprise, the small hand tightened around hers.

"Great! I'm so glad you can hear me. Now, if you're having any pain, squeeze my hand."

The hand in hers didn't move.

"Okay, then. You're going to be just fine. Rest now and let us take care of you."

Ethan frowned at her, then proceeded to perform another neurological exam. Kate wondered why he was upset with her. Had she done something wrong? For the life of her, she couldn't think of what.

Between them, they kept a sharp eye on Charlene's neuro status. Halfway to Trinity, she began to have respiratory problems.

"Her pulse ox is dropping." Kate double-checked the portable vent settings. "I wish we could listen to her lungs."

"Try hyperventilating her."

Kate followed Ethan's direction. "Think she threw a blood clot to her lungs?"

His troubled gaze met hers. "Maybe. From the look of her labs, she could be on the verge of DIC. Maybe she's septic as well."

"She's not running a fever, but that doesn't preclude the possibility," Kate agreed. "Should I give her another bolus of tPA?"

"Not yet." Ethan cued his mic. "Dirk, how soon will we arrive at Trinity?"

"ETA ten minutes," Dirk responded.

Ethan hesitated. "If her pulse ox doesn't improve with hyperventilation, we'll bolus her again."

Kate nodded, grabbing the Ambu bag. "I hope this works."

She disconnected Charlene from the portable vent and began giving her manual breaths with the Ambu bag. She and Ethan both watched the pulse oximeter readings. After ten breaths, the pulse ox hadn't budged one bit. Their patient still had dangerously low oxygen levels in her blood.

"Here, reconnect her to the vent and give the bolus." Ethan grabbed the vent tubing as he spoke, taking the Ambu bag connection off to replace with the vent tubing. "I'll increase her ventilator settings to continue providing a hyperventilation state."

Kate tossed the Ambu bag aside, then found a syringe and drew up the necessary dose from the tPA bag to give another bolus.

"Dirk, call Trinity and request a hot unload," Ethan directed.

"Ten-four. ETA five minutes."

Kate finished giving the bolus and then took Charlene's left hand, the unaffected one, in hers. "Charlene, squeeze my hand if you can hear me."

Nothing. Kate's stomach clenched. She tried again. "Charlene, open your eyes, squeeze my hand."

Still no response. Ethan pointed to the monitor. "Her blood pressure is dropping. I need you to start vasopressin."

Kate did as he'd asked, noticing how the helicopter banked to one side as Dirk began his descent. Kate had just gotten the medication tubing primed and connected when they landed.

Ethan jumped through the side door, going around the back to pull the patient out through the hatch. Kate guided the gurney from inside using her good arm to support it until Ethan and Dirk had control of the patient, then she leapt out to follow them.

They were met on the helipad by two emergency department staff members, a doctor and a nurse. Ethan shouted over the noise of the helicopter as they headed into the elevator. "We believe she threw a pulmonary embolus; we lost her oxygenation in flight."

Kate listened while the doctor and Ethan discussed several options. By the time they reached the emergency department, the patient was nearly in full cardiac arrest.

She watched helplessly as the nurse began doing chest compressions. Ethan shouted orders, and Kate followed the advanced cardiac life support algorithm, giving epinephrine while the doctor drew more blood. If Charlene did have a pulmonary embolus and the tPA infusion didn't dissolve the clot, there wasn't much more they could do.

Their resuscitation efforts ended all too quickly. For a long minute, after the doctor had called a halt to the proceedings and declared Charlene dead, Ethan simply stood there, staring down at her. Kate ached for him. She knew how difficult it was to lose a patient. Quickly she filled the nurse in, explaining how Charlene's husband and son were already on their way.

When there was nothing more they could do, Kate tugged Ethan's arm, drawing him away from the bedside. Every muscle in his body was tense as if he were hanging on by a mere thread. Despite knowing Dirk was waiting in the helicopter to take them back to Lifeline, she pulled Ethan into the empty staff lounge.

"What in the world happened? One minute she was squeezing your hand, the next she was dead." Ethan's sharp tone held a wealth of angst.

"She must've been bleeding internally. Before she threw more clots, especially to her lungs. Or maybe it was a clot that went to her heart. I'm sure the autopsy will tell us what happened."

"Where are your jokes and laughter now, huh?" Ethan snapped.

"This is the time for tears, not laughter." Kate didn't allow him to push her away. Instead, she stepped close and wrapped her arms around him. When she thought he might pull away, she held him close. "Ethan. I'm so sorry. I know how hard this must be for you."

For several seconds he remained tense as if he would yank away from her at any moment. But slowly his arms came up around her, and he bent his head, burying his face in her hair.

"She shouldn't have died." His whispered words were muffled against her hair.

Not sure if he meant Charlene or his wife, she tightened her hold. "I know. It's all right to cry, Ethan."

"I should have been there when she died." His voice was dull, flat. "I can't believe I wasn't there when she died."

This time, she figured out that he meant his wife. "You loved her, Ethan. That's all that matters." Helplessly, she tried to soothe him. Running her hands over his back, she pressed a kiss against his cheek.

He startled her when he turned and captured her mouth with his. She gasped he pressed his advantage, kissing her fully. What started as comfort quickly flared into something intense. Personal.

Wonderful.

His arms cradled her close. Kate couldn't think, couldn't breathe, her senses overwhelmed by the hot molten surge of desire. If there was a desperate edge to his kiss, she ignored it, the taste of him leaving her hungry for more.

He continued to press her close, drawing out the kiss as if there were no tomorrow.

"I hope someone made coffee—oops. Sorry."

Ethan lifted his head when the nurse barged into the lounge. He quickly dropped his arms and took a step back in retreat. Dizzy with need, Kate clung to the counter to stop herself from falling, willing her heart to slow down before she ended up on the wrong side of an emergency department bed.

He raked a hand through his dark hair, avoiding her gaze. "I, uh, we should get back."

Kate swallowed hard and nodded. She tried to gather her scattered thoughts. "Yeah, Dirk is waiting."

When Ethan turned away, she grabbed his arm. "Hey. I'm here for you if you ever want to talk."

He pulled from her grasp, his expression slamming shut

as if they hadn't just been lost in each other's arms. "There's nothing to talk about. Nothing can change the past."

"Maybe not, but you can change the future." Stubbornly, she trailed behind him as he strode out of the emergency department.

"Not for Charlene. And not for my wife."

Kate winced at the seemingly scraped raw and bleeding pain underlying his tone. She couldn't think of a suitable response, partially because he was right. There was no future for some.

But there was for Carly. And for Ethan, if he'd learn to give himself a break. She didn't know why he hadn't been at his wife's side when she died, but there must've been a good reason. How could she make him understand?

Maybe by focusing on his daughter, the one person he truly loved.

"Listen, Carly deserves a future, don't you think? Punishing yourself for the rest of your life isn't going to help your daughter." Or you, she silently added.

Ethan stabbed her with a quick, angry glance but didn't respond. She could only hope her comment had given him something to think about.

Because if she couldn't convince him to look forward, her plan to help him lighten up and enjoy life would be an abysmal failure.

7

"I have a surprise for you, Carly." Ethan glanced across the dinner table at his daughter, grinning when she cast him a suspicious expression of doubt. "Don't frown at me, this is a really good surprise. How would you like to go to an indoor waterpark in Wisconsin Dells with me and Kate? We are also bringing Tyler, a boy about your age. We'll leave early tomorrow morning and stay the whole day."

"Really?" Her tiny face brightened, then she frowned. "What's a waterpark?"

"A place with indoor pools and waterslides. There's even something called a lazy river where you can float on inner tubes."

"Oh, Daddy, that would be so much fun!" Carly jumped up from her seat and bounced up and down without the benefit of her Hippity Hop. "A waterpark. Do we get to wear our swimming suits?" When he nodded, she danced in a circle. In that moment, she reminded him of the way Kate had danced upon learning she wouldn't need surgery on her injured shoulder. "Goody, I can't wait!"

Her exuberance was infectious, making him glad he hadn't given in to the temptation of canceling his plans with Kate on almost a dozen separate occasions during the past few days. In the end, he hadn't made the call because he couldn't bring himself to disappoint his daughter.

It wasn't as if avoiding Kate was helping much anyway. The kiss they'd shared had rocked him, badly. He couldn't seem to shake the effect on his senses. He'd grown addicted to her kiss, craving a repeat performance to the point he obsessed about when he might have the chance to be alone with her again. He'd been so rattled he'd decided to ask a fellow female resident out for dinner, just to see if he felt the same earth-shattering sensation as when he'd kissed Kate.

He'd gone as far as approaching Gwen, who was model beautiful, but since he wasn't the least bit interested in kissing her, he chickened out at the last minute and had asked some lame work-related question instead.

Man, he had it bad. Ridiculous to put such emphasis on a simple kiss. Even if there had been nothing *simple* about kissing Kate. As much as he tried to tell himself any attractive woman would have made him feel the same way, after his failed experiment with Gwen, he couldn't bring himself to believe it.

Luckily, his and Kate's schedules had been crazy since the day he'd responded to her comforting embrace by pouncing on her. *Smooth, Weber, really smooth.* Although, truthfully, Kate hadn't seemed to mind. In fact, he could remember in exquisite detail how she'd responded.

Oh, yeah. She'd kissed him back.

He groaned under his breath and rubbed his hands over his face. These internal debates of his were driving him crazy. Only Carly's latest nanny prank had taken his mind off the kiss, at least temporarily.

He narrowed his gaze at his daughter, his expression turning serious. "Carly, you have to promise to stop being so naughty when I'm working. Secretly unraveling Mrs. Carter's knitting yarn and mixing up all the colors into one huge knot wasn't very nice."

Carly lowered her head and pouted. "It was only yarn, Daddy. She didn't get sick, not like Mrs. Vanderhoff."

Her five-year-old logic made his lips twitch. "Maybe not, but the yarn cost money, and she was knitting a sweater for her granddaughter." A granddaughter who would probably thank Carly one day for wrecking the thing so she wouldn't be stuck wearing it. "You still have several chores you need to do to help pay off your debt."

"I know." Carly let out a deep, heavy sigh as if she owed one million dollars instead of five bucks. "I'll help load the dishwasher."

"Okay." Ethan stood and began to clear the dirty dishes off the table. He'd cheated and stopped for fried chicken on the way home rather than cooking. The twelve-hour shifts he did at Lifeline were great in some ways, but he was never in the mood to cook by the time he got off work.

"Can we play a game, Daddy?" Carly wanted to know once she painstakingly helped him load all the dishes in the dishwasher.

"Ah, sure. What kind of game?" Warily, he eyed her. The most recent trip to the store had resulted in the purchase of two sponge arrow guns and matching goggles. No way would he ever be voted father of the year after buying his daughter a gun. But she'd been so excited, and he'd needed something good to distract her from the Silly String and Hippity Hop adventure.

"Let's play with the arrow guns!" Carly dashed off to her room to fetch the toys. For a moment, he was glad his wife wasn't here to see this. Susan would be horrified. He braced himself for the familiar flash of guilt.

Only, for some reason, it never came. Strange, but a sense of relief had replaced his constant guilt. Carly seemed to be doing better—in the past four nights she'd only had one nightmare. True, she still liked to terrorize her nanny, but even her pranks were getting more tolerable. Like she'd said, it was only yarn and at least Mrs. Carter hadn't gotten sick like Mrs. Vanderhoff had.

Kate had been right the night their patient, Charlene, had died. He couldn't go back and change the past, but he could have an impact on the future. Carly's future. Susan would expect him to, he knew that much for sure.

Splat. An arrow hit him in the chest. "Hey!" he protested. "Don't I get one of the guns first before you start shooting at me? And we need our eye protection, remember?"

"Okay, Daddy." She was already wearing her goggles, and the minute he had his on, she attacked again.

Carly's lilting giggles made him grin, and he chased her, dodging the harmless spongy arrows she sailed in his direction from both weapons. The echo of his daughter's laughter was well worth the stigma of buying a gun.

An hour and a half later, he tucked a happy Carly into bed.

"Did you tell Kate I want her to be my best friend?" she asked, snuggling beneath her blanket.

"Yep. She said she'd love to be your friend." Ethan bent down and kissed her forehead. "I want you to think happy thoughts about going to the waterpark tomorrow, all right? That way, you'll have sweet dreams."

Carly nodded her head. "And I'll think of Kate, too. She always cheers me up. I can't wait until tomorrow, Daddy."

"I know, sweetheart. Good night." Ethan pressed another

kiss on the top of her head, his chest welling with emotion. "I love you, honey."

"I love you, too, daddy."

Ethan left the door open as he always did, allowing the light from the hallway to spill into her room. In the kitchen, he opened the fridge and stared inside, then shut it again. He wasn't in the mood for a soft drink or for anything else. Restlessly, he prowled around the house.

This was the hardest part of the day, when there was nothing left to distract him from his loneliness. He glared at the television. He wasn't in the mood for stupid reality shows or a basketball game. He briefly considered checking out a movie on the subscription station they paid for each month, but he wasn't in the mood for that either.

He should use the time to start studying for his emergency medicine boards coming up in June, but he wasn't sure how well he'd be able to concentrate. Like his daughter, he was too keyed up over the upcoming trip in the morning. Especially because he'd be spending the day with Kate without a sick or injured patient in sight.

Finally, Ethan went to bed. But sleep didn't come easy. He couldn't relax. His mind wasn't helping, he didn't want to imagine Kate dressed in a swimsuit.

He tried to push the image away, although Carly's words echoed in his head. *I can't wait for tomorrow to come, Daddy.*

Oh boy, he knew how she felt because he could hardly wait for tomorrow to come either.

The next morning, Carly was wiggling so much Ethan could barely get her into her swimming suit, which she insisted on wearing beneath her clothes. Then he picked out dry clothing for her to wear and packed them along with swim trunks for himself, finally adding their beach towels to the pile. He was running late by the time he headed over to the Lifeline parking lot, where they were to meet Kate and Tyler.

He needn't have worried. Kate just happened to be running late herself. After a few minutes of Carly asking nonstop when Kate might get there, she pulled up alongside him in a cheery red car and rolled down her window. He could see a small, brown-haired boy belted in a booster seat behind her.

"Sorry I'm late. I had trouble getting a hold of my granddad."

Her tone betrayed her underlying anxiety. Was she looking for an excuse to back out? "Is everything all right?"

"Oh, sure." Her furrowed brow smoothed out. "He finally called me back. Everything is fine. Did you want me to drive?"

"My car is bigger, and I don't mind driving." Ethan figured it was the least he could do.

"Fine with me." Kate closed her window, pulled the key out of the ignition, and then gathered her bags. She opened her door, then the passenger door for the backseat. Tyler jumped out and walked right up to Ethan. "Hi. My name is Tyler O'Connor. Are you Dr. Weber? Where's Carly?"

Ethan's eyes widened. He'd always known Carly wasn't shy, but next to Tyler, she seemed downright timid. "Hi, Tyler. Carly's in the backseat. Give me a chance to get your booster seat latched in, and then you can jump in beside her. Ms. Lawrence and I will pack the rest of our stuff in the trunk, then we'll be on our way."

"Okeydokey." The minute they had the booster seat placed in the backseat next to Carly, Tyler climbed in. Ethan could hear the boy chattering away as he helped Kate store her bags in the trunk. He raised a brow when he saw the cooler.

"You brought lunch?"

She smiled. "Don't get too excited. It's mostly stuff the kids will like."

"Any food I haven't cooked is food worth eating," Ethan confessed. "Thanks. That was thoughtful."

Kate waved a hand. "No problem."

Ethan held the passenger door open for her, then jogged around the car to slide into the driver's seat. He pulled into traffic, trying to think of something to say. Why did this feel so much like a date? He'd agreed to this outing for the kids, a way to show Carly some fun and to give her a chance to spend time with her friend, Kate. Subtly, he swiped his damp palms on his jeans so they wouldn't slip off the steering wheel.

There was absolutely no reason to be nervous. This wasn't a date.

Thankfully, the kids chattered in the backseat enough that the stilted, polite conversation and long pauses between him and Kate weren't as noticeable.

"Did you hear the results from Charlene's autopsy?" Kate asked.

"No." He glanced over at her with interest. "What did it show?"

"You were right on the DIC. She had thrown clots to almost every organ in her body. The cause of death was listed as multiple pulmonary embolisms." Kate reached out and gently squeezed his arm. "I thought you'd want to know. We did everything possible to save her."

The news only brought a small measure of comfort. With all the great strides in medical care, he still felt as if he should have been able to do more. Thirty-six was far too young to die. "It's good to know what really happened. Thanks for telling me."

An hour later, he pulled into the parking lot of a well-known indoor waterpark called The Grand Adventure. Despite it being a Friday, rather than a weekend day, the parking lot was full, maybe because of spring break. Helplessly, he turned off the engine, not even sure what to do. He'd never been to a waterpark in his life.

"Grab our stuff from the trunk, will you?" Kate asked. "We buy our tickets inside."

"I'll follow you." He didn't mind being enlisted as a pack mule. He slung her bag and his over his shoulder and lifted the cooler. Kate took each of the kids' hands in one of hers and led the way inside.

"If we rent a room, we don't need to use the locker rooms and will have a place to store the cooler and eat lunch," she suggested.

"Sounds good to me. I'll pay for the room and the tickets." When she began to protest, he shook his head. "I insist."

He set down the bags and dug in his pocket for his wallet. After paying for the tickets and one of the very last rooms available, he led the way to the elevator.

It felt strange to be going into a hotel room with a woman who wasn't his wife. Ethan tried to remember they weren't here to spend the night, but the cozy atmosphere of the hotel room provided an intimacy that was difficult to ignore.

Thankfully, Kate was all business. After unpacking their clothes on one of the beds, she added ice to the cooler. When that was finished, she declared it was time to go. Like Carly, Kate and Tyler wore their swimming suits beneath their clothes. He quickly changed in the bathroom, feeling self-conscious in his black swim trunks.

Like Kate hasn't seen a bare chest before, he told himself

sternly. She was a nurse, which meant she'd seen many a human form. Feeling more and more like an idiot, he draped his towel around his shoulders and left the sanctuary of the bathroom.

Kate wore a royal blue modestly cut one-piece suit that wasn't nearly as tiny as his imagination had conjured up but bared enough of her golden skin that his mouth immediately went dry.

"All set?" she asked with a smile.

He could only nod and try not to stare. Get a grip, he lectured himself firmly. The four of them trooped back down to the waterpark as if they were a cozy family instead of a mismatched foursome.

Carly and Tyler immediately sprinted toward the biggest slide. Kate frowned. "She can swim, right?"

It took him a moment to realize Kate was asking about his daughter. He watched as Carly led the way up the ladder of the slide with Tyler at her heels. "Like a fish. Susan made sure she took swimming lessons," he responded absently.

"Good. Look, there she goes." Kate clapped her hands together as Carly sailed through the tube and hit the water with a big splash.

Ethan glanced at Kate, mentally whacking himself in the head for mentioning his wife's name. Kate hadn't seemed to notice. Her attention was centered on the kids.

"And there goes Tyler." Kate grinned when the boy followed Carly into the water. "That looks like fun."

"Really?" His tone was full of doubt. "I guess, if you're a kid."

"No, for us, too." Kate flashed a saucy smile and grabbed his hand. "Come on, don't be an old stick-in-the-mud."

"A stick-in-the-mud? Me?" Because it was probably true, he forced himself to follow Kate to the stairs for the slide.

He tried not to stare, but her backside was far too close as she began to climb. He told himself he was there for Carly, but the stirring of testosterone long-dormant made a liar out of him.

He felt like a fool, standing among the kids, waiting for his turn to go down the slide. When the time came, he felt a momentary hesitation. What if the stupid thing broke beneath his weight? Maybe the slides weren't meant to hold adults.

"Come on, what are you waiting for?" a particularly impatient kid piped up from behind him. "Don't be a chicken. You're holding up the line."

Ethan sighed and sat, feet first. Before he could blink, his bottom slid forward and he flew through the slick tube, the cold water beneath his back stealing his breath. Before he knew it, he crashed into the water with the tidal wave splash.

"Daddy, you looked so funny!" Carly shouted when he finally broke the surface. "Let's go again."

With a groan, he pulled himself out of the pool. Kate laughed along with Carly, her blond hair damp and slick. He had to fight the urge to pull her into his arms and kiss her senseless.

Reining in his crazy thoughts, he settled for a grin. "Sure, let's do it again."

For the next few hours, the adults followed the kids down their choice of waterslides. Ethan didn't want to admit he was having fun. Somehow the thrill of the slide managed to make him feel as carefree as a child.

Finally, Kate held up a hand in surrender. "Enough. It's time for us to relax in the lazy river."

"Absolutely." Ethan didn't hesitate to agree. The kids muttered about how boring the river was, but they reluctantly followed the adults, each finding inner tubes of their own to float in, spinning in wild circles ahead of the adults.

"Ahh, this is the best part," Kate murmured, leaning her head back on the edge of her huge donut-shaped inner tube.

"Yeah." Ethan was forced to agree. Instead of taking an inner tube of his own, he floated alongside her, keeping a hand on her tube to keep her close. "Kate, this was really a great idea. Carly's having a blast."

"So is Tyler." She raised a brow. "And what about you, Dr. Weber? Are you having fun as well?"

He pulled her closer so he could capture her hand in his. Leaning over, he pressed a quick kiss against the back of her hand, then allowed his gaze to travel over her. "Oh, yeah. I'm enjoying myself much more than I thought I would."

Kate's fingers trembled in his, and a pretty pink blush stained her cheeks. "Better watch your thoughts," she warned with a laugh. "This is a family establishment."

"Don't I know it. There are dozens of kids everywhere." He remained close, resting his forearms on her inner tube as they floated down the river. "I think next time you and I should go out alone to a nonfamily establishment."

"I'd like that."

Had she really agreed to go out on a real date with him? Before Ethan could ask her again, an older kid jumped from the side of the lazy river, miscalculating his aim so that he landed directly on top of them. Ethan lost his grip as Kate's inner tube capsized. He thought he heard her cry out before he sank beneath the water.

Frantically, he found his footing and stood, swiping water from his eyes as he glanced around for Kate. Where was she? Several empty inner tubes floated past. Was she under the water? He caught a glimpse of her blond hair and blue swimsuit, but his heart thundered in his chest when he realized Kate was lying facedown in the water, near the bottom a few feet from him.

"Kate!" He strode through the water and went down to grab and haul her upright out of the water. Her eyes remained closed, and she was limp in his grasp. Dear heaven, had she hit her head on the wall?

"Kate! Come on, Kate. Talk to me." Ethan lifted her, carefully setting her on the concrete edge of the lazy river. When he scrambled out to kneel beside her, his heart squeezed painfully as his worst fear was confirmed.

Her lips were blue, and she wasn't breathing.

8

———

Kate slowly became aware of two things: her head throbbed like a jackhammer busting up concrete and Ethan's lips were wonderfully soft yet firm against hers.

Ignoring the first was easy, but before she could appreciate the latter sensation to its fullest, her chest convulsed, and a lungful of water erupted from deep within. She pushed away from Ethan just in time to avoid spraying him in the face as she coughed and gagged on the water she'd inhaled.

How attractive, she thought with a wince as she struggled to breathe between hacking coughs. Poor Ethan. If seeing her like this didn't scare him off, nothing would. The pounding in her head intensified, and she reached up to massage her temple. Good grief, what had she hit?

"Easy now." To her surprise, Ethan didn't run in the other direction but held her shoulders supportively, bringing her head to rest against his firm, bare chest. The light sprinkling of dark chest hair teased her nose. "Breathe in, slow and easy."

"I'm trying." She gasped as another coughing spell ripped through her. After a few minutes, the musky scent of him penetrated the smell of chlorine, and she relaxed. The urge to bury her face in the curve of his neck was strong. As much as she wanted nothing more than to remain cuddled in his embrace, she lifted her head, belatedly aware of the crowd of people gathered around her. Carly and Tyler were both staring at her with wide, frightened eyes. With an effort, she smiled at them reassuringly. "Don't worry, I'm fine."

"You need to rest for a minute." Ethan didn't sound convinced. "Doctor's orders."

Carly and Tyler were still gazing at her fearfully, and she was hyperaware of Ethan's arms around her. Since when did she need comfort from others? She was the strong one, the one other people came to for help. Time to pull it together before she embarrassed herself further. "Why is it that doctors call what they do practice?" she asked in mock seriousness. "And how much practice do you need to get it right?"

A few of the bystanders chuckled, and the crowd slowly dispersed, convinced she would be okay. Ethan continued to frown at her. "This is serious, Kate. You hit your head on the cement side of the pool. You weren't breathing when I pulled you out."

"I'm sure it wasn't that bad, but thanks for rescuing me." She downplayed the danger, conscious of how intently the kids were listening. Didn't he know harping on the accident was scaring them? She turned her attention to the kids. "Hey, is anyone else ready for lunch? Carly? Tyler? Come on, I'm starving."

Ethan muttered something she couldn't quite hear under his breath, and she suspected it wasn't very nice. But when Carly and Tyler edged closer, he held his tongue as if finally realizing how in tune the two young children were with what had nearly happened.

"Are you really okay, Kate?" Carly's wide, frightened eyes tugged at Kate's heart.

She hauled the little girl close and gave her a big hug. "Of course, I am. I just swallowed a little water, that's all." Her headache mocked her, but she ignored it. With her other arm, she pulled Tyler into the embrace as well. "Come on both of you, let's go back to our room and unpack the cooler. I hid some treats in there for dessert."

Her diversion tactic worked. The kids scrambled away. She struggled to her feet, conscious of Ethan's warm, strong hand beneath her elbow. She loved his hands, the wide span of his palms, the strength in his fingers. From the very first she'd found Ethan physically attractive, but his protective caring was almost more than she could bear. If he didn't stop it, she'd have difficulty holding herself aloof, maintaining a friendly relationship.

The kids chattered as they all walked to the elevator, then began fighting over which one of them would push the buttons. Their room was on the fourth floor, so they agreed to compromise.

She found acetaminophen in her purse and took the extra-strength tablets for her headache. When it was time to unpack the cooler, the kids were more of a hindrance than a help. She'd thought her impromptu picnic-style lunch had been a great idea. Ethan remained serious and quiet; she could practically feel the tension radiate off him in waves as he opened sugar-free juice drinks and set them on the floor beside the kids.

"I have turkey, ham, and cheese sandwiches for us, peanut butter and jelly for the kids." She handed the food out as she spoke. Next, she pulled out a bowl of freshly cut fruit, a block of cheese, and a box of crackers. "Ethan, do you have a knife? I forgot to slice the cheese before leaving home."

Ethan searched his discarded jeans and pulled out a Swiss Army knife from the depths of a pocket. He opened the knife and handed it to her.

She held up the knife, raising a brow. "So, what do you think? Male or female?"

"Huh?" Ethan was clearly confused.

"This knife. Male or female?" When he still didn't get it, she waved it at him. "Male, of course, because it's useful enough for many things but spends most of its time opening bottles." She snickered at her own joke. Well, actually, her granddad's joke.

"You're crazy, you know that?" Ethan didn't so much as smile. "How can you make jokes at a time like this?"

"Why not?" Kate finished slicing the cheese, then offered some to the kids who were already munching on their sandwiches. "Dwelling on the worst-case scenario is unhealthy."

"Can we play video games?" Tyler had discovered two remote controllers connected to the television set. He held one in his lap and handed the other to Carly.

"No, I think there might be a charge for it," Kate cautioned. "Besides, you need to finish your sandwich first."

"I did finish my sandwich," Tyler protested.

"Me, too," Carly added.

"Go ahead, Tyler, the charge doesn't matter." Ethan gave his permission, then turned back to Kate. He lowered his tone so the kids wouldn't hear. "I don't agree. Ignoring something this serious is just as unhealthy. You could have died."

"But I didn't. Thanks to your quick reflexes." She

mustered a smile. "Ethan, the one thing my granddad taught me was the value of laughter. Awful, tragic things happen every day, it's true. But when the worst doesn't happen, we should celebrate and be thankful. We should enjoy what we have with humor. Carly and Tyler are already scared enough. We don't need to make this any worse for them."

"I know." His voice was low, and he stared at his half-eaten sandwich as if his appetite had completely vanished.

"Your daughter needs laughter in her life," she pointed out softly. "And so do you."

"It's been hard since Carly's mother died," Ethan finally confessed. "Especially since I was working late doing an extended surgical case when she died. When I got home, I felt so lost, confused. She'd died peacefully in her sleep, but Carly and I were wrecks. How can a person even think of humor when seeing your daughter in agony?"

"I know it's not easy to laugh when you're hurting. Crying is good, but there comes a time when crying doesn't help anymore."

"Easy for you to say, your daughter didn't lose her mother." Ethan's tone held a trace of bitterness.

"Maybe not. But when I was eighteen, I lost my best friend. His name was David O'Malley. We were so close, had been friends throughout grade school and into high school, supported each other through various dating fiascoes." Kate could still picture David, tall with closely cropped red hair and a temper to match. Ten years had passed since he died, but at times, it seemed like she'd just seen him yesterday. "One day, he didn't show up for school. Normally, he'd have called me, even if he was sick. Since he didn't, I headed over to his house right after class."

She hesitated. Painful memories dive-bombed from all directions, but she forced herself to finish the story. "I found him in the garage with all the doors closed and the car running. I opened the garage door, pulled him out, and started CPR, having learned the technique in school, but it was too late."

"I'm so sorry." Ethan's dark expression was full of compassion. "I can't imagine how awful you must've felt."

"It was rough. He left a note. He said goodbye to his parents, his older brother, and to me, his only friend." She could barely push the words past her constricted throat. "I couldn't believe he would do such a thing. Then I couldn't believe I hadn't known how down and depressed he must've felt." She helplessly tossed the rest of her sandwich aside, crumpling the empty bag in her hand. "That's what haunts me still. That I didn't know."

"Kate." Ethan reached out and took her tightly fisted hand in his. "Depression is a serious illness, and you were only eighteen. How could you know?"

He was only telling her the same thing she'd heard from the psychologist she'd gone to see after David's death, but she couldn't make herself believe it. Not deep down where it counted. She slowly opened her hand and entwined her fingers with his. "Anyway, I was in bad shape afterward. My granddad couldn't stand to see how depressed I was becoming, so he took me to his place to live with him."

"Your granddad sounds like a great guy."

She smiled, squeezed his hand, then drew hers away. Distance. She needed distance from this new, compassionate Ethan, or she'd throw herself into his arms and refuse to let go. She steadied her tone. "He is. You'd like him. Anyway, he worked on me for months, trying to make me smile, then eventually teaching me how to laugh. I know it's not easy. But it's important, Ethan. For you and for Carly. Especially for Carly."

"You're right, I know you are. In here . . ."—he tapped his temple—"I know what I need to do. Feeling up to it here . . ."—he touched his chest—"is another matter."

She poked him playfully in the ribs, making him chuckle. "Lucky for you, I know all kinds of silly jokes to lighten things up. You'll be amazed at how much I can help. Some days, I spend hours surfing the Internet for joke sites." Kate glanced over to where the kids were having a great time with the video games. She raised her voice to be heard over the sound of race cars on an obstacle course. "Dessert anyone? I think there are brownies hiding in the cooler."

"In a minute," Tyler said.

"Hey." Ethan stroked a finger along the back of her hand, and the tingling sensation drew her attention as fast as if he'd stripped naked and danced on the table. "Thanks for telling me about your friend."

She was touched that he'd picked up on the fact that she hadn't told many people about what had happened ten years ago. She smiled. "You're welcome."

Digging in the cooler, she pulled out the brownies that she'd stayed up late last night to bake. She carefully unwrapped the generous squares and handed one to each of the kids and Ethan. When he raised a questioning brow at her, she gave in and took a healthy bite of the fourth brownie. The smiles and obvious enjoyment helped make her feel better.

This trip was meant to be a way to introduce a little fun into Ethan's life, but instead she'd been conked on the head, nearly drowned, and had bared her darkest secret.

And now she feared the line of friendship between them was already blurring beyond recognition. Worse, she didn't care. For once, she wanted to do something for herself regardless of the consequences.

Even if those consequences meant that letting go of Ethan after he and Carly didn't need her anymore would be the hardest thing she'd ever done.

ETHAN FIGURED if anyone deserved the Ironman award for maintaining control, it was him. Swimming, biking, and running was easy compared to surviving the day without touching Kate, like really touching her, or more, giving in to his desire to pull her close and kiss her until they both couldn't breathe.

Yeah, he was quite the gentleman, all right. If not the Ironman award, then maybe the Boy Scout Badge of Honor? Surely, he deserved something for getting through the entire day without completely losing his mind.

Darkness had fallen, cloaking the car in a veil of intimacy as he drove along the non-crowded interstate highway toward home. The kids had fallen quietly asleep in the backseat, exhausted from hours of swimming and food. He figured the dent in his checkbook had been paid back double by the sound of Carly's laughter and her rapt expression of enjoyment.

He glanced at Kate, seated beside him. It hadn't taken long for her to tip her head back, resting against the seat, and fall asleep. She was quite the woman, bouncing back from her near-death experience with hardly a whimper. Those moments when he performed rescue breathing for her had seemed endless, but she'd brushed off his concern. Her head was no doubt throbbing, not to mention her shoulder, which she hadn't murmured a single complaint about either. No, instead, she'd spent the afternoon trying to make him laugh with her goofy jokes.

A smile tugged at his mouth. He couldn't think of anything except seeing her again, without Carly as a chaperone. But how to broach the subject? How long since he'd been out on a date? Years. Many years. He and Susan had been married for five years, getting married while he was in his second year of medical school, and they'd dated for two years prior to that. And she'd been gone for about a year now.

His gut twisted, and he tightened his grip on the steering wheel. Nine long years. All right, so maybe he was out of practice. Things couldn't have changed that much. All he needed to do was simply ask Kate out. For dinner. Or a movie. He frowned. There must be nice restaurants around here someplace, even if he couldn't name one that didn't include a children's menu. What movies were playing? Were any of them any good? He had no clue. He'd need to ask around for advice.

Far too soon, he pulled into the Lifeline parking lot, where Kate's car was waiting.

He gently shook her arm, waking her. Blinking, she lifted her head and quickly glanced in the backseat.

"Don't worry, they've been out for quite a while," he assured her.

"I guess I was, too. But thanks to my nap, my head already feels better." She smiled. "Thanks for a great day, Ethan. I'd better get Tyler home. Shelly is going to wonder if we kidnapped him."

When she moved as if to get out of the car, he put a hand on her arm. "Kate, I'd—that is . . . Would you like to go to dinner sometime?"

He could have kicked himself for being vague, but for the life of him, he couldn't remember her schedule or, for that matter, his. He held his breath, waiting with insecure agony for her reply.

"Sure, I'd love to."

"Great." Relief washed over him. "I need to find a babysitter for Carly, so I'll need time to work something out."

"I understand. No rush. Whatever works for you."

No rush? In his opinion, tomorrow was too long to wait. And her seemingly cavalier attitude made him frown. Still, they were both scheduled to work in the morning, so finding a sitter by tomorrow evening was out of the question anyway, especially at the last minute for a Saturday night. He hoped they wouldn't have to wait another whole week for their date.

"Great. I'll see you tomorrow." Before he could talk himself out of it, he leaned forward and brushed his mouth against hers. He'd been dying to kiss her all day, and mouth-to-mouth resuscitation didn't count.

His intention had been to keep things light, but she met him more than halfway. His pulse skipped when she kissed him back. His ego was soothed by her fevered response.

Just as quickly, she pulled away, slightly breathless. "See you in the morning."

Kate darted out of his car and unlocked hers. While she started her car to warm up the engine, he pulled the sleepy Tyler out of the back seat and held him while Kate unlatched the booster seat so she could place it into her own vehicle.

The rest of the supplies were moved without fuss, and soon she drove off with a little wave.

Ethan stared after her for a long moment and resigned himself to the truth. Carly wanted Kate to be her best friend, but he wanted something far more. Desire zipped along his nerve endings like a wildfire feeding off dry grass.

Man. The idea of a real relationship tempted and scared him more than seeing Kate lying pale and lifeless in his arms.

He could only hope he didn't get burned.

9

Ethan entered the debriefing room a few minutes before the start of his shift.

"There's an ICU transfer waiting for a flight to Trinity Medical Center," Reese informed him as he headed straight for the counter where the coffee was located. With a sinking heart, Ethan realized the coffee maker was empty. Belatedly, he remembered Reese wasn't a coffee drinker, but considering the four hours or less of sleep he'd gotten last night, Ethan would have paid fifty bucks for one full pot.

"Is Kate here yet?" He tried not to gaze longingly at the empty carafe. If only he had five more minutes to make even a half a pot . . .

"I'm here." Kate's cheerful presence arriving at that moment dashed his hopes of making coffee while they waited for her. "Good morning. I hear there's a flight waiting. Why didn't the night shift crew go?"

"The call came in a half hour ago, but there was some glitch on the part of the accepting physician," Reese explained. "Everything is fine now, though."

"Okay." Kate nodded. "Anything going on with the weather we need to know about?"

"Clear and cold, very little wind and no fog." Reese summed up their flight status concisely. "If you guys are ready, let's roll."

"We are," Kate answered for both of them, although when Ethan grimaced, she sent him a questioning look. As they followed Reese out to the hangar, she fell into step beside him. "Are you all right? You look awful."

"Gee, thanks. I needed to hear that." He spoke dryly. "Don't worry about me, I'm only suffering from caffeine withdrawal. What do we know about our patient?"

"Not much." They reached the chopper and climbed aboard. "I'll fill you in after takeoff."

Ethan settled into his seat and pulled his helmet over his head. He watched as Kate strapped herself in as well. Despite his fatigue, he was thrilled to be flying with her today. He could honestly admit he didn't regret having walked away from his surgical residency a little over a year ago. Every shift on the Lifeline chopper brought a new challenge. Emergency medicine suited him far more than he'd ever realized.

He cued his microphone, listening as Reese communicated with the paramedic base. Apparently, they were heading to Plainville Hospital, located just south of Green Bay, so he knew at least that much. He grinned when Reese smoothly lifted the helicopter into the air. Planes were fine, but the real flying was like this, in a chopper, rising perpendicularly from the earth and turning on a dime.

He loved it.

"Our patient is a sixty-five-year-old woman who was hospitalized with severe pneumonia, which quickly turned into Acute Respiratory Distress Syndrome." Kate's voice in his headset caught his attention.

He nodded, all too familiar with the syndrome. ARDS was an unfortunate yet relatively common complication of pneumonia. The problem was that once ARDS set in, weaning a patient was often extremely difficult, requiring a lengthy ICU stay.

And often resulted in death.

"So why the request for a transfer?" he asked.

Kate reviewed the sketchy notes left from the night shift. "Apparently, our patient lives here in Milwaukee, and her granddaughter is a nurse at Trinity. Per the granddaughter, Plainville Hospital cannot meet her grandmother's complex medical needs."

"Ah, I see. The granddaughter pulled strings." Not that Ethan blamed her. If his grandmother was still alive, he'd pull strings to get her transferred to Trinity, too. He stifled a yawn. Man, what he wouldn't give for some coffee.

"What's wrong? You look frazzled." Through the shield of her helmet, Kate's eyes were deeply green and luminous with concern.

"Carly woke up around two in the morning from a bad nightmare," he admitted. "I didn't get back to sleep until four thirty, and the alarm went off at five fifteen. So yeah, I guess I didn't get much sleep. Nothing new."

"A nightmare? About what?"

Rats. Ethan shifted uncomfortably in his seat. If his brain had been firing on all cylinders, he wouldn't have mentioned the nightmare. Now he couldn't think of a way to avoid the truth. "She, ah, dreamed about you. At the pool."

"Oh, Ethan." Kate audibly gasped. "She had a nightmare about me? Almost dying?"

Grimly, he nodded. Carly had awoken, screaming for

Kate, repeating over and over again, *Don't die, Kate, please don't die!* Until he managed to wake her up and assured her that Kate was fine.

"How awful. The poor thing. Ethan, you need to get her a dream catcher."

A frown wrinkled his brow. "A what?"

"A dream catcher. The Native Americans believed that hanging a dream catcher above your bed draws all the bad dreams out of your head." At his incredulous expression, she sadly shook her head. "I know, you don't believe in such fairy tales. Why am I not surprised? Can't you just put logic aside for a while and go with the flow?"

"A dream catcher has nothing to do with logic or going with the flow."

Kate let out a snort. "Did you ever once think that Carly's mischievous behavior could be related to her need to believe in fairy tales? A need for her to believe her hopes and dreams have a chance to actually come true?"

"I don't know." How did they get from Carly's nightmare to psychoanalyzing his life? Defensive now, he frowned. "I read her stories. *Cinderella* is a fairy tale."

"But you don't believe in having a happily ever after." Kate's voice was confident. "I bet you barely hide your cynicism."

"I'm not cynical, for Pete's sake." He sighed. This was far too intense a conversation after a night of broken sleep and no morning coffee. "I'll look for a dream catcher, all right?"

Kate settled back in her seat with a satisfied expression on her face. "Great idea. Why didn't I think of that?"

Ethan inwardly groaned. Thankfully, Reese interrupted them. "ETA ten minutes."

"So soon?" Kate's voice held surprise. "They didn't call us with report."

"Forgot to mention, the doctor was called to another emergency. He asked if he could give you an update when you arrive," Reese informed them.

"We don't seem to have a choice. I hope the patient is stable enough for a transfer," Kate said in a wry tone.

Ethan silently echoed her sentiment. There was nothing worse than being told one thing, then arriving at the hospital to find a completely different picture—usually for the worse. He understood that smaller hospitals didn't have as many resources as large, academic medical centers did. But transport companies like Lifeline didn't appreciate losing patients en route.

It tended to be bad for business.

Reese landed the helicopter, and Ethan made sure he was the first one off so he could pull the gurney out of the back without Kate's help. She hadn't mentioned her shoulder injury, but he suspected she was still bothered by it. Although, she hadn't let it stop her from enjoying the waterpark yesterday. She also hadn't allowed her near drowning and head bruise to interfere with her determination to have fun either.

He followed Kate's lead, having never been to this hospital before. She knew where the ICU was located, and they were quickly escorted to their patient's bedside.

"Oh no." Kate's eyes widened in shock when she reached the bedside. "What's her name?"

"The patient?" Ethan glanced at the armband around the woman's wrist. "Lucille Johnson. Why?"

"Not Miranda? Are you sure?" She bent forward to review the name on the wristband for herself as if she didn't believe him. "Good. Her name is Lucille, not Miranda. That's good."

"Are you all right?" It was Ethan's turn to be

concerned. Maybe the bonk on her head had been more serious than he'd thought. "I take it she looks like someone you know?"

"Yes, but I'm fine. Sorry. My mistake. I'll get her transferred onto our equipment." Kate busied herself with the various cables and tubing.

Ethan turned his attention to a harried physician who approached. "Dr. Lane? I'm Dr. Weber. Can you fill me in on Lucille's care?"

"Certainly." The young doctor looked familiar, and Ethan wondered if the guy had graduated in the class ahead of him. He listened intently as Dr. Lane gave him details about the woman's medical course including the various antibiotics she'd received. Lane also showed Ethan the most recent set of blood gases, along with her vent settings. After a few minutes, Ethan concluded the patient, while still too hypoxic for his peace of mind, was probably stable enough to fly.

"I wish her oxygenation was better," Ethan murmured to Kate, showing her the most recent lab results. "But we should be all right to transport."

"Yeah, her blood gases could be higher, too," Kate agreed. She programmed the last IV pump, then turned toward him. "I'm ready when you are."

"All right, let's go."

Ethan took the brunt of pushing the patient—luckily, she wasn't very heavy—as they made their way to where Reese waited in the helicopter. Kate stepped forward as if to help lift the gurney through the hatch, but Reese met them outside the chopper, grasping her arm and shaking his head. She backed off, and Reese took over the job of helping Ethan lift her into the back hatch.

When they were finally airborne, Kate cued her mic.

"My shoulder is much better. There's no reason for you to keep babying me."

"Have you gone to see the orthopod yet?" Ethan asked.

"No." Kate narrowed her gaze as if daring him to argue.

"I'm not going to let you lift until you're cleared by the orthopedic surgeon." Why was it that doctors and nurses made the worst patients? Talk about not complying with her doctor's recommendations. He wanted to shake her until her teeth rattled. When she opened her mouth, he held up his hand. "No. You know Jared will back me on this, Kate."

"Fine. I'll make the appointment."

She was clearly irritated with him, so he busied himself with their patient. Probably not a good time to ask about her schedule to see when they could go out on a real date. He was off tomorrow, Sunday, but Carly had school on Monday morning. His spirits sank. There were all sorts of preparations to make before a school day, which made him think he might not be able to finagle a date until the following weekend.

Kate's normally cheerful expression was still pulled into a frown as she worked. It didn't bode well for him. Even once he managed to figure out a day he could get a babysitter and ask Kate out, he could only hope she hadn't changed her mind.

KATE KNEW she was acting like a child, but she couldn't help being annoyed with Ethan. Wasn't she a flight nurse with medical knowledge? Shouldn't she be the judge of her shoulder pain? What would a doctor, especially an orthopedic surgeon, tell her anyway? Nothing except to rest and to try not to strain the joint until the pain was gone. You didn't need an MD behind your name to figure that out.

Much of medicine was good old-fashioned common sense.

Her irritation with Ethan helped her to ignore the eerie physical resemblance between Miranda, Granddad's new girlfriend, and the woman stretched out on the gurney before her. True, she'd only met Miranda the one time, but she wondered if Miranda had a sister named Lucille.

She made a mental note to ask her granddad the next time she spoke to him. It troubled her that Granddad had been acting odd lately, and she was pretty sure Miranda was partially the reason. First of all, the first few times she spoke to him, he hadn't had any jokes to share with her, which in itself was abnormal. Then, on two separate occasions, she'd made plans to get together with Granddad, only to have him cancel at the last minute with some vague excuse she didn't for one minute believe. She understood he had his own life and deserved to be happy, but since when had these transient women kept him from spending time with his family?

Since never.

Until now. Until Miranda. She mentally scowled. Maybe she needed to have a heart-to-heart with her granddad. This strange behavior was concerning. She wanted to get to the bottom of it before it was too late.

Too late for what, she wasn't sure. All she knew was that the idea of her granddad falling deeply in love with someone he'd barely known for a few weeks bothered her.

"Kate?" Belatedly, she realized Ethan was speaking to her. "Did you hear me? I said her pulse ox is dropping, and I increased the oxygen on her ventilator to seventy percent."

"Got it." She made a notation on the flight record. "Seventy percent is pretty high."

"Yeah. I know." Ethan's voice was husky through the headset, and she noticed his hand rested protectively on the patient's frail shoulder. "I hope her sixty-five-year-old heart can take it."

His compassion eased her annoyance. Ethan was so different from the first time she'd flown with him a little over ten days ago. He was much more likely to smile, even if he wasn't exactly overwhelmingly appreciative of her silly jokes. She even heard him laugh once or twice.

The line of friendship had been crossed, though, with their kisses. Her cheeks grew warm when she remembered how much she'd enjoyed his embrace. She hadn't had any serious relationships with men over the last ten years, pretty much since David's death. She'd been tempted a few times before, but not like this. Especially not with a resident who would only be around for a couple of months.

Still, the riotous emotions Ethan stirred in her were difficult to control. Would it be so bad, she wondered, to allow the relationship to stray down a different path? One where she didn't have to keep him at arm's length for the sake of her mission?

She shivered. This was uncharted territory for her, and she didn't know how to proceed. Or what the consequences might be. What if things didn't work out between them? What if Ethan regressed as a result and all of her work was for nothing?

So far, her plan was working beautifully. Ethan was less serious and willing to do the right thing for Carly, even to the point of buying her a dream catcher when he didn't believe in them.

Why, then, was she willing to sacrifice what was already working so well? And soon Ethan would be well on his way to a happier life with his daughter, and neither of them would need her at all.

If she were strong, she would resist the temptation of Ethan's mind-drugging kisses. A relationship wasn't worth the potential loss of the ground in her ability to rescue Ethan Weber from himself.

The knowledge didn't offer comfort. Instead, it swirled through the hollow, gaping hole in her gut.

KATE HUNG on to her resolve to do the right thing, even while working alongside Ethan. Lucille grew agitated shortly before they were due to land, and she had to grab the woman's hand when she wiggled through the strap around her wrist.

"Hey, now, don't try pulling a Houdini," Kate said to their patient. Little old ladies tended to be the best at magically getting out of their safety straps. She glanced at Ethan. "Do you think she needs something for pain, or do you think this is a result of her hypoxia?"

"I'm not sure. Give her two milligrams of morphine and we'll see how she reacts." Ethan shook his head with a wry smile. "I don't know what it is with you and agitated patients. You seem to draw them like a magnet."

"Tell me about it." Kate suspected in this particular case thinking about Ethan's kisses was partly to blame. "Reese, how soon until we land?"

"ETA seven minutes," Reese responded. "Are you all right back there?"

"We're fine," she assured him.

They were able to transfer the patient to Trinity Medical's intensive care unit without any problem. She and

Ethan made sure their patient was fine before they headed back to the helicopter.

Thankfully, the day continued to be busy, with one call after another. Kate was glad for the distraction from her wayward thoughts. Finally, toward the end of their shift, things slowed down.

She concentrated on completing her paperwork, telling herself she was not avoiding Ethan. He sought her out, though, as she finished the last of her reports.

"Kate. I, uh, need to ask you something."

His serious expression made her stomach clench. She braced herself. "Yes?"

"I just called home. Apparently, Carly is in rare form again. She's hiding behind the furniture and shooting sponge arrows at our newest nanny." The corner of his mouth twitched as if he were tempted to smile, but somehow he managed to maintain his serious expression. "I need to go straight home, so I won't have time to stop and buy the dream catcher you mentioned." He cleared his throat and shifted awkwardly. "I hate to ask anything more of you, but would you mind picking one up? I can get it from you during our next shift—we both work on Monday."

"Of course! I don't mind," Kate assured him. "Don't give it a second thought."

"Thank you." His voice lowered, sending ripples of awareness down her spine. "I owe you one."

"You don't owe me a thing. You saved my life, remember?" Kate quickly turned away to file her report in the proper folder because every instinct she possessed made her long to throw her arms around Ethan and kiss him. She forced a carefree attitude. "Besides, I'm always happy to help out a friend."

He frowned as if not liking that reference, but the arrival

of the oncoming shift forestalled further conversation. Kate followed Ethan into the debriefing room, eager to report off and then leave.

Forty-five minutes later, she was holding a beautiful dream catcher in her hand, the light in the store glittering off the beads that dangled from the carefully woven circle. At the counter, she hesitated. If she waited until Monday to give Ethan the dream catcher, Carly wouldn't have it for the next two nights. What if the little girl suffered another nightmare? Ethan would go another two nights without sleep.

She paid for the gift, then headed out to her car, bending her head against the nippy wind. How would Ethan feel if she brought the gift over tonight?

Kate started her car and drove toward the interstate. She knew Ethan's address, had seen it listed next to his phone number during the time she'd worked on the schedule for Jared. She'd noticed because Ethan's house wasn't very far from Lifeline. Stopping there on her way home wasn't out of her way.

She drummed her fingers on the steering wheel and wrestled with her thoughts. No way did she want to barge in on Ethan at home, yet the thought of Carly facing another night filled with nightmares nagged at her. The child's welfare was the most important thing here. Right? Right.

Before she could change her mind, Kate drove to Ethan's house, battling a mixture of wary determination and thrilled anticipation.

10

Spring in Wisconsin could be brutal, Kate thought as she stood in icy wind and stared at Ethan's front door. Finding his house hadn't been too difficult, she'd recognized his car in the driveway. But now she doubted the wisdom of coming. How would he react to her spur of the moment visit?

Her concern over Carly having another nightmare was the only thing that gave her the courage to press the doorbell. Within moments she heard heavy footsteps, then the door opened.

"Kate!" Ethan wore a surprised expression, although he opened the door wide. "Come on in."

He was dressed comfortably in a thin, long-sleeved green T-shirt, well-worn jeans, and moccasins. He looked great and smelled even better. An irresistible combination.

"I'm sorry to bother you, but I brought a gift for Carly." She held up the pretty pink gift bag to show him. "I hope she isn't asleep."

"No such luck," Ethan said wryly. He raised his voice, "Carly! Kate is here to see you."

"Kate's here?" Carly dashed in from where she must've been brushing her teeth in the bathroom, given the dab of neon blue toothpaste staining her pink Barbie flannel nightgown. Without warning, the little girl threw herself at Kate, clutching her tightly around the waist. "I'm so glad to see you."

"I'm happy to see you, too." Kate awkwardly bent to return the hug, smoothing her hand over Carly's shiny blond hair. The silken strands were still slightly damp as if Carly had recently gotten out of the bathtub. She pictured Ethan painstakingly brushing his daughter's hair and smiled. There was no sign of the pink Silly String, and she imagined he'd spent a long time getting the stuff out of Carly's hair.

"Hey, give her a chance to breathe why don't you?" Ethan's teasing tone was the perfect way to lighten the mood. "Carly, why don't you take Kate into the living room so she can sit down?" He turned to Kate. "What can I get you to drink?"

"Um, whatever you're having is fine." She could barely think when he looked at her like that, so intensely, as if her comfort was the most important concern on the planet. Carly relaxed her viselike grip but tugged on Kate's hand, pulling her toward the sofa.

She sat down, then handed Carly the gift bag. "I have a special present for you, but it's not a toy or anything to play with," she quickly cautioned, hoping the little girl wouldn't be disappointed.

"I love presents," Carly announced. She snuggled onto the sofa alongside Kate, then dug through the pink tissue paper. Carly gently pulled out the dream catcher, holding the woven eighteen-inch circle up by the loop on the top.

The little girl's wide gaze was full of appreciation. "Aww, it's so pretty. Thanks, Kate."

Kate smiled, secretly impressed at her polite tone. Ethan had done a great job raising his daughter. "Aren't you going to ask me what it is?" Reaching out, she lightly touched one brightly colored feather hanging from the bottom of the circle.

"It's a hangy thing, right?" Carly pointed to the woman painted in the center of the circle. "She looks like an Indian."

"Actually, she is a Native American," she corrected. "This is a dream catcher, Carly. The Native Americans are smart; they know that sometimes kids like you have nightmares." Kate took the braided circle from Carly's hands. "See this woman in the picture here? She'll be watching over you, and whenever a bad dream comes, she'll catch it and hold on to it before the bad dream can reach your mind."

"Really?" Carly's wide eyes, so like Ethan's, were full of hope.

"Yes, really." Kate stroked the feathers dangling from the bottom of the circle. Ethan entered the living room and set a soft drink on the table beside her.

"But how do you know it works?" Carly's lower lip trembled.

"Because I had one when I was a girl." Kate met Carly's gaze straight on and kept her tone matter-of-fact. "I used to have lots and lots of nightmares, just like you. Then one day, my granddad bought me a dream catcher. I thought he was crazy, but he hung it over my bed anyway. And you know what? It worked. I didn't have any nightmares with the dream catcher hanging over my bed. The dream catcher caught each one."

"Let's go hang it up in my room right now!" Carly

jumped to her feet and grabbed Kate's hand, tugging urgently, clearly eager to test the theory. "Come on."

Kate laughed. "All right, but I think we're going to need your dad's help, too." She met Ethan's gaze over Carly's head, silently begging him not to scoff at the dream catcher idea.

"I think it's a great idea to hang it up right now. I've got some tools in the kitchen." He momentarily disappeared into the other room as Kate followed an impatient Carly into her bedroom.

Kate imagined Carly's room might have been designed by her mother, but she could easily imagine Ethan painting the white fluffy clouds on the pastel pink walls and the dozens of yellow stars on the ceiling. The room was absolutely perfect for a little girl like Carly.

"See if your dad can put a nail or something up there." Kate gestured to the area of the ceiling directly above the head of Carly's bed. "Then the dream catcher will hang about here." She indicated the space with her hand.

"Can you do that, Daddy?" Carly asked when Ethan entered the room.

"Here, let me step up on Carly's bed." Ethan stood on the mattress and touched the star on the ceiling. "Is this where you want it?"

"Perfect." Kate nodded.

"All right, then." He deftly screwed an I-hook into the ceiling, then threaded clear nylon through the loop. "Hand me the dream catcher."

Kate held up the braided circle, and he put one end of the nylon rope string through the loop, then tied it to the other end so the dream catcher dangled about two feet above Carly's pillow.

"Thanks, Daddy." Carly clapped her hands excitedly.

"Thank Kate, this was her idea." He gazed at the Native American woman painted on the inside of the circle for a long moment before turning back to his daughter. "Now, it's really late, Carly. Time for bed."

"I know." Carly nodded as if she had planned all along to go to bed without a problem. "Can Kate help tuck me in?"

"Sure. Crawl in, and I'll give you a hug and kiss good night." Kate drew back the covers so Carly could get beneath them. Then she bent down to give the child a hug and kissed her cheek. "Good night, Carly. Sleep tight."

"Good night, Kate." Carly yawned widely. "Thanks again for the dream catcher."

"You're very welcome."

"Wait for me in the living room, would you?" Ethan murmured as Kate moved past him toward the door.

She nodded, then left him alone with his daughter. In the living room, she stood awkwardly. The room was comfortable, toys strewn about as if Carly had played with them recently. A very healthy sign, at least in her opinion. Houses where kids played shouldn't always remain neat and clean.

She crossed the room and picked up the soft drink Ethan had provided for her. The root beer was sweet and tangy on her tongue. Her muscles tensed when Ethan walked down the hall and into the room.

"Thanks for waiting." He grinned one of his killer smiles. "And thanks for bringing the dream catcher. I really hope it works."

"I hope so, too. All it takes is a little willingness to believe." She took another sip of her root beer.

Ethan gestured to the sofa. "Please, sit down."

It was a bad idea. She already felt way out of her depth,

being in his house with him. Oh, sure, Carly was right down the hall, but that didn't make this feel any less intimate.

He must've sensed her hesitation. "Please? You have no idea how long it's been since I had a non-work-related, adult conversation."

She sat, mostly because her knees went weak. "We talked at the waterpark all day yesterday," she protested.

"I know. And I enjoyed myself, at least up until the part where you hit your head and nearly drowned." Ethan sat next her, his lean, denim-clad legs brushing lightly against hers. She inwardly groaned, regretting the fact that she was still wearing her flight suit. Couldn't she have run home first and dressed a little more nicely? No, because that would put too much meaning into this little impromptu visit. Which was for Carly's benefit, not hers. Or Ethan's.

Pull it together, Lawrence. She forced a smile. "I'm glad. I wanted you to have fun."

"Did your granddad really buy you a dream catcher when you were eighteen?" He eyed her doubtfully over the rim of his root beer.

"Yeah, he did. And before you ask, the dream catcher did work for the most part. The nightmares came far less frequently after he hung it up for me."

"Maybe you subconsciously were over the worst of them anyway," Ethan countered.

"Maybe. Does it matter? Isn't the most important part that Carly believes?"

He sat back against the sofa cushions. "I suppose you're right. I'd do anything, even standing on my head and singing the national anthem, if I thought I could chase her nightmares away."

Kate giggled. "Please. I'd love to see that."

A wry grin tugged at his mouth. "I'm glad you stopped over tonight, Kate."

He was? She took a gulp of her root beer so fast she nearly choked. "I'm glad, too. You both could use a good night's sleep. Maybe Carly won't wake up tonight."

"I hope she won't, but that's not why I'm glad to see you." He reached out and tucked a strand of her blond hair behind her ear. "I like spending time with you."

Oh boy, she was in deep trouble now. Her pulse raced, and her head felt distinctly wobbly. With an effort, she set down her root beer, careful not to spill any. "I like spending time with you, too, Ethan. But really, it's late and you must be exhausted. I should go." If she were smart, she'd run as fast as she could.

"I'm not that tired." As if he sensed her inner struggle, he pulled her close, his voice husky. "Don't go."

She couldn't have moved even if she'd tried. Ethan eased her into his arms, giving her all the time in the world to pull away.

She didn't. The first brush of his mouth against hers was tentative, the soft caress wasn't nearly enough. She wanted so much more.

"Ethan." She breathed his name, her hands splayed against his chest. There was nothing to interrupt them this time. No way to pretend this kiss wasn't happening.

"You are so bright, so beautiful." He cupped her cheek with his palm, holding her gently as he leaned forward to kiss her again. Being held by Ethan felt so right. She hadn't ever gotten close to one of her projects before.

Not like this.

The kiss went on for several long moments. She felt a little like they were a couple of teenagers. Only instead of their parents coming in to find them, they had to worry about Ethan's daughter looking for a glass of water. The thought made her laugh.

Ethan raised his head, his eyes dark with emotion. "What's so funny?"

"Nothing." When his gaze narrowed, she hastily explained, "All right, if you must know, we're funny. I don't think I've ever spent time on the sofa kissing a boy since I was, well, eighteen."

Uncertainty flashed in his eyes, and she immediately regretted her thoughtless comment. "I don't have anything against it, mind you, except, well, I keep looking over my shoulder, expecting my granddad or my parents to find us."

"Or my daughter." Ethan dragged a weary hand through his hair, putting a little distance between them. "I'm sorry."

"Don't be sorry." She leaned forward and kissed him again. "But it's probably better if we take things a little slow."

He laughed without humor. "Slow. You're killing me, you know that, right?"

Kate wanted to burst out laughing again, but she knew that Ethan wouldn't appreciate why she thought this was funny. Instead, she tipped her head to the side and regarded him thoughtfully. "I'm sorry."

He let his breath out in a rush. "No, don't be silly. I'm the one who's sorry. I'm being a jerk. You have every right to take things slow."

"Ethan." She hesitated, unsure what to say. She didn't want to let on that this was new territory for her. That she'd never been in a romantic relationship with a man she'd taken on as a project before. Especially not with someone she worked with.

"Kate." He mimicked her tone, then brought her close for a quick hug. "Hey, cut me some slack, I'm new at this." The teasing note vanished from his tone as he added, "I don't want to mess this up with you, Kate. I really don't."

Her resistance melted into a tiny puddle at her feet. "You haven't messed up, Ethan. You mentioned getting together for dinner. Would you like to come over to my house tomorrow night? I'll cook."

A slow smile tugged at his lips. "Yes, Kate. If I can find a babysitter, I'd love to come over for dinner."

"Good." Kate had no idea what she'd make for him, but at the moment she didn't care. "Around six?"

"I'll be there." He gave her another quick kiss. "Thanks for inviting me."

Rational thought fled from her mind, and it took every ounce of her willpower to pull herself out of his arms. "You're welcome. Seriously, Ethan, I need to go."

"Of course." He stood and offered a hand. She allowed him to draw her upright. "Come on, I'll walk you to the door."

Kate firmed her willpower as he walked her toward the door. Somehow, she managed to make it out to her car without falling flat on her face.

She drove home, wondering how she'd manage to make dinner for Ethan when she didn't really know how to cook.

THE NEXT MORNING, Kate was up at the crack of dawn, poring through every cookbook she owned. Granddad had bought a half dozen of them for her over the years.

She could use Granddad's advice now. He was the one who reveled in entertaining the ladies. Surely, he'd have an opinion on what recipe would be a good one for her to tackle.

She waited at least until nine in the morning before calling. Anxiously, she paced the living room with her cell phone at her ear while she waited for him to answer.

When he did finally pick up, he sounded breathless. "Hello?"

"Granddad, it's Kate. I didn't wake you up, did I?"

"Eh? What? No, of course not. I'm awake." Although he'd denied she'd woken him, he didn't sound like his usual jovial self.

"Are you sure you're all right, Granddad?" Kate couldn't put her finger on it, but something seemed off. "Is something wrong?"

There was a slight hesitation before he answered. "No, there's nothing wrong. Don't you think I'd know to call you if there was?"

"I guess so." He sounded cranky, which only made her think something really was going on. It was on the tip of her tongue to ask if Miranda was there, but sanity overruled her impulse. She did not want to know. "By the way, does your lady friend Miranda have a sister named Lucille?"

"No, she is a brother named Henry." Granddad's tone was tart. "Why do you ask?"

"Never mind." Kate shook her head at her ridiculous thoughts. Miranda wasn't some woman who'd changed her name from Lucille looking for a rich man to get her hooks into. Even if she was, her granddad was too smart to fall for something like that. And seriously, she had to stop watching so much television. No more *Dateline*. "Listen, Granddad, I need a favor."

"What's that?"

"I need an easy recipe for dinner. I sort of invited a friend over for dinner. A man."

"A man, huh? Well, there's always takeout."

"I'm serious." Kate scowled and continued to pace. "Please? There must be something easy for me to make."

"Hmmm. How about grilling a couple of steaks? Can't go wrong with serving a guy meat. And if it makes you feel better, you can throw in a salad."

He wasn't helping her in the least. "It's freezing outside, despite being early April. I'm not grilling steaks. Will you please think about it and call me if you come up with any ideas?"

"Sure. What time is dinner?"

"Six o'clock."

"All right, I'll think about it and call you back," he promised.

"Thanks. And, Granddad?" Kate headed back toward the kitchen. "When are we going to get together? How about tomorrow night? I would be happy to drive over to visit you after work."

"Um, sure. Tomorrow night will work out fine. See you later." He disconnected from the call. She stared at her cell phone for a moment before setting it aside. Granddad was acting stranger and stranger. Since when was steak his dinner of choice? He loved pottering around in the kitchen and usually always had a wealth of ideas.

If she didn't know better, she'd think he was trying to get rid of her. Because of Miranda? Because his woman friend was over there this very moment?

Kate groaned and buried her face in her hands. She did not want to think about her granddad's love life, not when his was so much better than her own.

She sighed and lifted her head, staring at the clock over

her microwave. Nine-oh-five. Only eight hours and fifty-five minutes until Ethan would arrive, expecting a home-cooked meal.

Maybe Granddad's idea of takeout wasn't such a bad one after all.

11

Ethan ran a finger along the inside collar of his shirt, trying to loosen his tie. Maybe wearing a dress shirt and a tie had been going a little overboard, but what did he know? This was his first date in nine years, and he was way out of practice.

Yet he was also full of anticipation. He didn't want to take one moment for granted.

He stepped onto Kate's porch. He rang the bell, then shifted the large bouquet of flowers into his other hand, lifting the other to adjust his tie. The stop at the florist had also reinforced how out of touch he was. Had there always been so many kinds of flowers to choose from? Shying away from traditional roses, he agonized for several long moments, then settled on a bouquet of yellow and pink tulips. They were bright and sunny and soft, instantly reminding him of Kate.

She opened the door, greeting him with a wide, welcoming smile. "Hi, Ethan."

She wore sleek chocolate brown slacks and a soft gold sweater that hugged her curves. A lump formed in his throat, and he thanked his lucky stars she'd invited him over. He crossed the threshold, handing her the flowers. "Hello, Kate."

"Oh, they're beautiful." She immediately buried her face in the blooms. "Thank you."

"You're welcome." He sniffed the air appreciatively, the scent of basil, oregano, and other Italian spices making his stomach growl. He glanced with interest at his surroundings. He hadn't been surprised to find that Kate lived in a quaint side-by-side townhouse. When he first met her, he'd gotten the impression she was seeking a good time, but he soon realized her openly friendly behavior was really a result of her cheerful attitude toward life in general and not because she was into the party scene.

His ears burned with embarrassment when he remembered how he'd accused her of coming on to him. At least she'd forgiven his rude behavior.

Kate's living space was homey and bright, filled with family pictures and comfortable furniture. Splashes of bold colors, blue, green, and purple, somehow managed not to clash. A scrawny tabby wove around his legs.

"Hello there." He reached down to scratch the feline behind its ears.

"Monty will hound you all night for attention if you keep that up," she warned, heading toward the kitchen. "I'm putting these in water."

The cat meowed when he followed her into the kitchen.

"Would you like something to drink?" She glanced at him over her shoulder. "I have root beer and diet cola."

"Root beer is fine."

"Great." Her cheeks were flushed, and she set the flowers on the counter, then opened the cupboard overhead. She pulled out two tall glasses, then filled them with ice cubes.

After filling the glasses with root beer, she handed him one. "Thanks again for coming."

"Thanks for inviting me."

"These are gorgeous, Ethan." Kate set her soft drink aside and fussed with the flowers for a few minutes before setting them prominently on the counter. "How did you know tulips are my favorite?"

He shrugged one shoulder. "I didn't, but they reminded me of you."

"Oh." She blushed, and he found himself smiling at her nervousness. At least he wasn't alone.

"Something smells great."

"I made chicken marsala." She took another sip of her soft drink before pulling on a pair of oven mitts. "Dinner should be ready any minute."

He watched as she drew a glass baking dish from the depths of the oven, along with a loaf of fresh Italian bread. The oak kitchen table was set for two, complete with tall candles in the center of the table. Ethan was suddenly glad he brought the flowers and had worn a tie. Clearly, Kate had gone out of her way for him.

"Something I can do to help?" He leaned his hips against the counter, content to watch her.

"Slice the bread, if you don't mind." Kate set a serrated knife and the warm bread on the cutting board next to him.

He did as she asked. It was nice to spend time with her in the kitchen. By the time he'd finished, she had filled two plates with food and set them on the table. She scooped the slices of bread into a basket, then gestured to the table. "Please, sit down."

"Do you mind if I light the candles first?" He'd found a lighter in the drawer next to the silverware.

"That would be nice. I hope you like Italian," she murmured as he pulled out the chair across from her.

"Everything looks great." He wished she would relax. Tension was radiating from her in waves.

"I have a confession to make." Kate lifted wide, anxious hazel eyes to his. "I'm not exactly an experienced cook. This whole meal"—she gestured to the table—"is a complete experiment."

"Really?" He raised a brow and eyed the table warily. "It doesn't look like an experiment."

"Eat at your own risk," was her solemn response.

He laughed and took a bite. The chicken may have been a little on the dry side, but he'd cut his tongue out before mentioning it. The marsala sauce was tangy, and the bread was wonderful. "Everything is excellent," he declared.

"I hope so." Kate tentatively took a couple of bites, tasting her own meal. "Hey, it's not too bad," she said in surprise.

"Maybe you should cook more often," he teased.

"Are you kidding?" She flashed a horrified glare. "Do you know how much work this is?"

Ethan leaned over to capture her hand in his. "Yes, and I want you to know I appreciate your efforts. You didn't have to cook, I would've taken you out."

"I know." She held his hand and gazed at him. "I just wanted to do something special for you."

His heart stuttered in his chest, and he suddenly found it difficult to swallow. His voice dropped. "You have. Thank you."

He couldn't remember what else they talked about as they ate. Kate's words tumbled through his mind, and he was humbled by her desire to impress him. He wanted to do the same for her, and when she stood and began to clear the table, he stopped her.

"Don't worry about this now." He took the dirty dishes from her hands. "Why don't you sit and relax while I clean up? If there's one thing I've learned over the years, it's how to wash dishes. I'm a pro."

"Absolutely not." She gently pushed him aside, then covered the leftovers with foil. Before he could start running water in the sink, she steered him away. "Neither of us are going to waste time with dishes. Come on, let's go for a walk."

"A walk?" He glanced around in surprise. "Outside?"

"Of course, outside." She laughed. "Where else did you expect we'd walk? On a treadmill? Together?"

The image was ridiculous, but still. "It's cold out," he warned as she fetched her coat.

"I know. We don't have to go far. Come on, the fresh air will be great."

He tried to maintain some enthusiasm as his vision of sitting beside her on the sofa, picking up where they left off the other night at his house, faded from his mind. With a sigh, he put on his jacket. She'd slaved over a meal for him. If Kate wanted to walk, they'd walk.

Their breath fogged the air in front of their faces as they headed down her driveway. Ethan wrapped his arm around her shoulders, protecting her from the worst of the wind. "Are we walking any place in particular?"

"Down the street to the park. There's a swing set and a little merry-go-round."

"Kate, I'd like to point out that we're finally alone without a little kid in sight—why on earth are we going to the park?"

"Because it will be fun," she insisted. "You're too serious, Ethan. Come on, just for a few minutes."

"Okay." Scary, but in that moment, he realized he'd do anything to make her happy.

True to her word, the park wasn't far from her place. She broke away from his grasp and ran toward the swing set.

"Give me a push," she commanded.

He came up behind her and lightly grasped her hips. Obligingly, he gave her a push, and she giggled as she swung in the air. Shaking his head at her enthusiasm, he gave her another push. The only female he'd pushed on a swing had been Carly. Susan was not the type of woman to play like a kid.

It was sobering to realize just how different Kate was from his deceased wife. He'd loved Susan, she was a great wife and mother, but Kate was like a breath of fresh air.

And it struck him how much he needed her to breathe.

"This is great. You should give it a try."

"I'll take your word for it." He intended to give her another push, then changed his mind. Instead, he caught her swing and held it, slowing her momentum. Wrapping his hands around her waist, he pulled her close and lowered his mouth, seeking the softness of her neck.

"No fair." She caught her breath when he kissed her.

"Did I ever promise to play fair?" He continued to hold her as he explored the delicate curve of her jaw with his mouth. Her skin tasted better than any dessert.

"Ethan." His name was little more than a whisper.

He wanted her with a fierceness that caught him off guard. They were in a public park. She was on a swing. What was he thinking?

"Kate." He drew in a lungful of cold air, hoping to clear the desire from his brain. He walked around until he stood in front of the swing. He took her hand in his and drew her to her feet. "You're driving me crazy."

"I am?" She leaned toward him, and he couldn't prevent himself from stealing another kiss. "In a crazy good way or in a crazy bad way?"

He groaned. "Both. Good crazy and bad." He pressed a kiss to the tip of her icy nose. "We'd better walk before we freeze to death."

She gestured toward the merry-go-round. "One more quick ride and we can go back."

He shouldn't have been surprised. Kate jumped onto the merry-go-round and laughed when he spun her in a circle. Despite his thinking this a foolish way to spend their time, he found himself jumping on the merry-go-round to join her. Oddly enough, he found himself having a wonderful time being with her like this, outside on the merry-go-round.

When Kate grew tired of the merry-go-round, they wandered back to her townhouse. He reminded himself that this was their first date. And even though he wanted to spend more time with her, he needed to find the strength to restrain himself.

Hopefully, there would be other dates. He needed to take things slow and easy.

Outside her front door, he hesitated. Temptation would be easier to resist if he didn't go inside.

"Ethan, I had a fabulous time tonight."

"Me, too." Even though he knew it was tempting fate, he found himself asking, "Do you mind if I come in? Just for a few minutes?"

"Oh, um, sure." She looked surprised but held the door open so he could follow her inside. "I thought you'd have to get back to Carly."

"I do, but it's not quite eight o'clock yet." He'd told the babysitter he'd be home by ten at the latest.

After removing their coats, Kate took a seat on the sofa, leaving him little choice but to sit beside her. He struggled to think of something to say, some topic that would distract him from his desire to kiss her again.

"How did the dream catcher work?"

"Great." He didn't want to talk about Carly or the dream catcher. He wanted to talk about them. Where this bubbling attraction between them was headed. But he couldn't find a way to put his thoughts into words.

And if he were honest, he'd admit that teetering on the brink of a relationship with Kate was downright scary.

He'd been married for a long time. Was it fair for him to rush into this?

It wasn't. But he hadn't felt like this before with any other woman. He'd loved Susan, but this was different.

Exciting.

Oh boy, he'd made a mistake coming inside like this. He wanted nothing more than to kiss her senseless again, and it took every ounce of his restraint to keep from reaching for her.

"Listen, Ethan, I don't want you to get the wrong idea here . . ." her voice trailed off.

He sensed she was warning him off and knew it was the right thing to do. The chemistry between them was impossible to ignore.

He cleared his throat. "I'm not getting any ideas, Kate, I promise. I enjoyed your dinner very much, but you're right. I should head home to Carly."

Her wide eyes were a deep purple, a color he hadn't seen yet. "I understand that you need to leave."

He didn't want to, but he absolutely had to. Before he

lost all semblance of control. He was a man, not a machine with an on-off switch. Yet, at the same time, he was incapable of hurting her.

Lifting his hands, he cradled her face. "I want to thank you again for cooking for me." He kissed her, trying to let her know without words what he was feeling.

"You're welcome. I'm just glad the meal turned out okay."

"It was the best meal ever." He gently kissed her again, then forced himself to release her. His feelings were rising and swelling in his chest to the point that if he didn't get out of there fast, he was going to make a fool of himself.

"I'm sure it wasn't, but thanks."

He told himself to leave. Now. Before he said something that might scare her off, for good.

KATE PULLED herself together with an effort. She thought that riding the merry-go-round with Ethan was enough to make him relax and enjoy himself. But afterward, the emotion swirling in his eyes had been a bit overwhelming.

Inviting him to her place had been a bad idea. She should've known better than to get personally involved with one of her projects. Ethan was learning to smile and laugh. Carly was doing better, too.

It was clear they didn't need her anymore. It was time for the two of them to move on. To find someone who would make their family complete.

Someone other than her. She wasn't the type of woman men wanted to settle down with. And that was okay, she was sure she'd find a new project.

She watched as Ethan shrugged into his coat, then

walked him to the door. "Thanks for coming." Her voice sounded falsely cheerful to her own ears.

"Kate, I'd like to see you again, sometime soon." His low husky voice reminded her of all the things she couldn't have. She wanted nothing more than to throw herself into his embrace, but she crossed her arms over her chest as a way to stop herself from acting like this was more than it was.

"Okay, sure. It would be fun to get together, maybe with the kids next time. Say hi to Carly for me."

"Kate, please—" He raked a hand through his hair as if struggling internally with something. "I don't want to rush you, and I know we've only known each other for a short time, but you need to understand how much I care about you. In fact . . ." His voice trailed off for a long moment before he added in a rush, "I think I'm falling in love with you."

Whoa. Wait. Love? Had she heard him correctly? No, it couldn't be.

Men didn't fall in love with her. They moved on to other relationships.

Ethan couldn't possibly love her. Could he?

The abrupt jangle of her phone interrupted her thoughts. She was tempted to ignore it, but then realized with a sinking sensation that the ring tone was the one she used specifically for her grandfather.

"Excuse me, I need to get that." She turned away from Ethan and picked up her cell phone. "Hello? Granddad, is that you?"

"Kate?" Her granddad's familiar voice flowed over the line, although it was soft and faint. "Do you have time to come over?"

"Of course, but why?" His tone sounded off, and all her senses when on full alert. "What's wrong?"

"I—don't know." Granddad's voice faded, and she strained to hear him. "I think I need help, Katie girl—" The sharp clatter of the phone hitting the floor on the other end of the line pierced her ear.

"Granddad!" she shouted. "Granddad, can you hear me?"

"Kate, what's wrong?" Ethan immediately crossed over to her, taking the phone from her limp fingers.

"Granddad needs me. He's sick." Her emotions were in a turmoil. She tore herself away from Ethan, rushing over to grab her coat. What on earth had happened? A heart attack or stroke? What were his symptoms? Had he blacked out? His heart. Oh, no. What if it was his heart?

She turned to find Ethan on the phone. He caught her gaze and lifted a hand. "Just a moment, I'll get someone who has the address." He handed her the phone. "I called nine-one-one, but they need your granddad's address. You talk while I drive."

Kate didn't argue but gratefully accepted his help. She gave the address of her granddad's house to the nine-one-one operator, then gave Ethan directions on how to get there. Once the dispatcher had sent an ambulance to her granddad's, there was nothing more she could do but sit back and pray.

Please, God, don't take my granddad. Not yet. Please? I need him so much!

12

———

Kate stared blindly out the window at the blur of scenery flashing by. Helplessly, she clutched her fingers into fists, wishing Reese or Nate could swoop down in the Lifeline chopper, pick them up, and fly them to her granddad.

Ethan pulled into the driveway about the same time the wail of a siren could be heard growing louder as the ambulance approached. He'd barely stopped the car when she opened the door and jumped out.

"Granddad!" Thankfully, the front door was unlocked, and she barreled through, her gaze searching for her grandfather. "Where are you? Granddad?"

The living room was empty, so she dashed into the kitchen to find him slumped over the kitchen table, his cell phone lying on the floor at his feet.

"Oh, no! No!" She thrust her arms beneath his and lifted his seemingly frail body up and off the chair, setting him gently to the floor so she could examine him properly. As she aligned his airway, she felt Ethan come up behind her. "I don't think he's breathing."

"The paramedics are here; they'll have all the equipment we need." Ethan's steady, take-charge tone helped remind her of the times they'd flown together and had cared for patients together. "Let's start CPR."

She'd already given Granddad two breaths and was feeling for a pulse. She couldn't feel anything, but she didn't trust yourself either. Her own heart was racing so fast it was difficult to concentrate. Ethan knelt across from her, placing his fingers on her granddad's carotid artery.

"No pulse," he said. "I'm starting chest compressions."

Kate heard him begin to count just as there was the clatter of footsteps running into the house. Two paramedics entered the kitchen, shoving the kitchen table out of the way so they could get better access to Granddad.

"Here." One of them handed her an Ambu bag and oxygen mask. "Use this while we get him hooked up to the monitor."

With trembling fingers, Kate fit the apparatus over her granddad's nose and mouth, then waited as Ethan counted his compressions. When he reached fifteen, she gave her grandfather two big breaths.

"He's in V-tach. We need to shock him. All clear!"

Kate let go of the Ambu bag, knowing that if she didn't, electrical shock could transmit through the material to her. The second paramedic had just finished placing an intraosseous IV in Granddad's femur, hooking up the IV tubing before letting go.

"Shock him three times, then give him a loading dose of amiodarone," Ethan directed.

The paramedics did exactly as he told them. She bit her lip hard when that jolt of electricity jerked through her granddad's seemingly frail frame. She felt every one of the shocks as if the defib pads were pressed to her own chest. On the third shock, his heart rhythm finally converted.

"He's in first-degree heart block with PVCs," the first paramedic stated. "Hooking up the loading dose of amiodarone now."

"Does he have history of heart problems?" one paramedic wanted to know as the other began to insert a breathing tube.

Kate averted her gaze, swallowing hard. It was more difficult than she'd ever imagined watching Granddad being treated like a patient. She forced the words past her tight throat. "Yes. Three years ago, he suffered a mild heart attack. They placed a stent in one of his coronary arteries. I think it was the right descending artery."

"Surgery?" Ethan asked.

"No, he didn't need surgery." Not then. But somehow she feared he'd need it now.

If he survived long enough.

"Blood pressure is better, ninety-six over forty." The paramedic glanced at her. "We'll need to transport him to the hospital ASAP."

"Will you please take him to Trinity Medical Center," Kate begged. "I used to work in the ICU there and that's where Granddad's doctor is."

"Will do." The paramedics didn't need her assistance. Helplessly, she watched as they quickly transferred Granddad to the gurney and wheeled him outside.

"I'll drive you to the hospital, Kate." Ethan followed her out, putting a hand on her arm.

"No, I want to ride in the ambulance with him." She turned to the paramedics, who exchanged a long glance. "I'm a nurse. I promise I won't be in the way."

"Kate, let me drive you." Ethan's hand tightened on her arm.

Ignoring him, she wrenched from his grip and pinned the paramedic with a hopeful look. "Please?"

"Sure, you can ride along." When the paramedic granted his permission, Kate didn't waste a second giving him a chance to change his mind. She jumped in the back of the ambulance behind Granddad.

Just before the doors closed, she caught a glimpse of the hurt expression on Ethan's face. Because she'd pulled away from him after he'd said something about falling in love with her? Honestly, she didn't really believe him. Ethan must know that his daughter needed to be his top priority.

As soon as Ethan faded from sight, she turned her attention to her granddad. Watching and praying he'd be okay.

When they reached Trinity Medical Center, Kate couldn't follow him all the way into the trauma room. She watched as the paramedics discussed his care with the emergency department physician, who had already called in the cardiology team.

Kate waited in the lounge because they took her grandfather directly to the cardiac cath lab. They had her granddad in there for almost half an hour before someone came out to talk to her.

"Kate Lawrence?" She nodded and jumped to her feet when the resident approached. "Your grandfather has three completely blocked arteries, the original one that was stented three years ago, along with two more. He is on his way to the operating room for a three-vessel bypass."

"Three vessels." Kate's knees gave way, and she collapsed down onto the chair. "Open heart surgery."

"He'll be fine, he's holding his own at the moment." The resident awkwardly patted her shoulder. "If you want to head over to the operating room waiting area, the surgeon, Dr. Elliott, will come out to talk to you when the procedure is over."

There wasn't any place else to go, so she followed the resident's suggestion. The waiting area was a large room with sections portioned off for privacy. A few other people were already there, but she wasn't in the mood to talk, so she found a private corner and sat down.

Open heart surgery. The words echoed over and over in her mind. She scrubbed her hands over her eyes. As a student nurse, she watched an open heart case, fascinated by the entire process—the way they were able to bypass the heart in order to operate on it, the detailed work the surgeons did, grafting the arteries.

She slammed her eyes shut. Her memory was far too good. She didn't want to imagine Granddad lying on the cold, hard OR table with his chest open and some surgeon cutting into his heart. She didn't want to think about the myriad things that could go wrong. She knew all too well that complications happened during scheduled open heart cases. Clinically, she knew an emergency procedure held more risk.

How many emergency heart cases actually survived? She had no idea.

Her parents. Kate pulled herself upright and dug out her cell phone. She needed to call, to let them know what happened. Where were they exactly? She stared blankly at the phone realizing she had no clue. She hadn't memorized their European cruise itinerary. Helplessly, she dropped the phone back in her purse. Maybe she'd wait until he was out of surgery, then she'd be able to share good news on how well he was doing.

The alternative was too painful to contemplate.

When she grew tired of sitting, she stood and paced. Horrible coffee from the nearby vending machine was her only choice, but she downed a few cups anyway until every nerve in her body jittered so badly it was a wonder she didn't leap out of her skin.

The hands on the clock moved in slow motion. She stared at the time, trying to think back. They'd gotten to the hospital with Granddad around 9:15 at night. Then he'd gone to the operating room around ten.

It was only 10:40 now. Granddad wouldn't be out of surgery for another two to three hours.

Maybe longer if things didn't go smoothly.

Feeling completely alone, she plopped back into a chair and cradled her head in her hands. She knew Ethan probably would've stayed with her, at least for a short while. How long had he arranged to have the babysitter stay with Carly? She had no idea.

The wounded expression in his eyes when she'd left him outside Granddad's house haunted her. It must have felt like a slap in the face after he'd confessed falling in love. Why had she left him there? Why couldn't she accept his willingness to help?

Was he really falling in love? With her?

Panic seized her by the throat. No, he couldn't have developed feelings for her already. Theirs was a temporary relationship. Two friends, out to have fun.

Until she'd blown it by kissing him. She crossed the line of friendship and didn't know what to do. Her throat closed, and tears welled in her eyes.

What was wrong with her?

"Kate?"

She lifted her head and opened her eyes, sniffing inelegantly. She blinked away the tears because she thought it was Ethan standing in front of her. Except he had to be home with Carly, who had school in the morning.

But the blurred version of Ethan sat beside her, using his thumb to brush away a single tear. "Hey, don't cry. Your granddad's going to be fine. Dr. Elliott is a great cardiothoracic surgeon. You couldn't ask for anyone better."

"I know." She sniffled again and glanced around in confusion. "Ethan, what are you doing here? Where's Carly?"

"I made arrangements for her to stay at a friend's house overnight—that's what took me so long." He offered a lopsided smile. "We had everything packed, were practically out the door, when she insisted we go back because she wouldn't leave without your dream catcher. She's very impressed with how well it's been working."

Uncharacteristically, fresh tears threatened. What was with the waterworks? Kate was forced to admit she was an emotional train wreck. "That's so sweet."

"Yeah, Carly really likes you."

She'd meant the fact that he'd gone to such lengths to be there with her at a time when she needed him the most, but she couldn't find the words to tell him.

"Kate—" Ethan drew her name out in a sigh. "Don't cry. I don't have any tissues."

"I do." She dug one out of her purse and blew her nose. She drew in a deep breath and let it out slowly. "I'm sorry. I don't know what's wrong with me."

"You're worried about your grandfather, that's what's wrong with you." He reached over and placed a comforting arm around her shoulders. "I understand."

"Why are you being so nice to me?" Kate simply couldn't comprehend his actions, not after she'd left him so abruptly. Not only had he come back, but he made arrangements for

Carly to spend the night at a friend's house, just so he could be with her as long as she needed him.

His expression softened. "You know why, but this isn't the time to get into a heavy discussion about our future. So, what else can we talk about? Hmmm." He pretended to think. "Hey, maybe you should give Jared a call. I'm not so sure you're going to be in any condition to work tomorrow."

"Neither are you if you stay here with me. Granddad could be in surgery for hours yet." Kate had considered calling Lifeline earlier but had given up the idea. "I can't call off for tomorrow, we're short staffed enough as it is. Besides, once Granddad is out of surgery and in the intensive care unit, there isn't anything else I can do for him. I can come and visit once I'm off work."

Ethan remained silent for a few minutes. "I'm not leaving you here alone, so if you're going to work tomorrow, then so am I. Maybe we'll have a slow day. We can hope for fog, or a whopping snowstorm."

She gave a weak laugh. "How about a tornado? Although, April is a little early for tornado season."

"Yup, and Wisconsin is too far inland for a hurricane."

His dry response almost made her smile. "Oh, Ethan." Kate leaned into him, dropping her head onto his strong shoulder. "I'm so glad you're here."

"Me, too." He pressed a kiss to the top of her head. "I'll always be here for you, Kate."

She didn't know what to say to that, so she fell silent. Amazing how much easier it was to sit patiently in the waiting room with Ethan's arm around her. Listening to the strong, resonant beat of his heart beneath her ear, she knew he'd meant what he'd said.

He would be there for her as long as she needed him. But she wasn't good in long-term relationships. The one and only guy she'd loved had taken his own life rather than talk to her.

She squeezed her eyes tight and shunted those thoughts down another path. Like she'd told Ethan, they couldn't change the past, but she could focus on the future. Granddad would need her more than ever once he made it through surgery.

She'd be there for him the way he'd been there for her.

"Kate?" Ethan gently stroked her cheek. "The surgeon is here to talk to you."

"Huh?" Blinking owlishly, she lifted her head, wincing at the crick in her neck. She must've dozed. "I'm awake."

"Ms. Lawrence?" Dr. Elliott took her hand in his. "Anthony Lawrence has been transferred to the Cardiac Intensive Care Unit. You will be allowed to visit once the nurse gets him settled."

"How is he? How did the surgery go? Any complications?"

"He's fine. Overall, surgery went well, although I did have some trouble controlling his blood pressure. I still have him on vasopressors."

Kate nodded, knowing vasopressors post heart surgery weren't uncommon. Frankly, his condition could be much worse. "He's not bleeding or anything?"

"Not that I'm aware of." Dr. Elliott's expression was wry. "Don't worry, I plan to head back inside to check him over before I head home."

"Thank you." She held his hand tight for a long moment before releasing it.

"You're welcome." He smiled at her, then nodded at Ethan before heading out of the room.

"He's out of surgery." Kate sat down, feeling dazed. "He's going to be fine."

"Yes, he is." Ethan glanced around the now empty waiting room. "Should we go down to the cafeteria for something to eat?"

"No." Kate wasn't leaving until she'd seen Granddad with her own eyes. "I'm not really hungry."

Waiting to hear from the ICU took longer than she expected. Almost an hour passed before a nurse phoned through to the waiting room, asking for her.

"Dr. Elliott wanted to wean him off the vent, we just took out his breathing tube," the nurse explained in a rush. "I'm sorry about the long wait."

"That's all right. You've really weaned him off the ventilator that quickly?" Kate could hardly believe it.

"We did. Come in and see for yourself."

Kate hung up the phone and turned to Ethan. "They've already extubated him. Will you come up with me to see him?"

"Of course." He slid his arm around her waist as they headed for the elevator.

The lights in CICU were low, but the staff nurses were still busy even after midnight. The unit clerk behind the desk directed her to Granddad's room.

"He's awake, but very groggy," the nurse warned. "I've just given him a couple milligrams of morphine for pain."

Kate nodded, approaching his bedside with a wide smile on her face. She would be cheerful if it killed her. "Granddad?" She reached for his hand. "I'm so glad to see you."

Her grandfather opened his eyes and tried to speak. She couldn't understand what he was saying.

"It's okay, don't try to talk. Just rest, Granddad. You're going to be just fine."

He shook his head as if frustrated, then tried again.

Rather than watching him struggle, she leaned close, straining to hear. "Miranda."

"Miranda?" Kate straightened, her gaze perplexed. "You want me to call Miranda?"

Her granddad closed his eyes and nodded wearily.

"All right, Granddad, I'll call her," she promised, knowing the woman's number was likely in his phone.

She was shocked that Miranda was the first person her grandfather had asked for. Clearly, his lady friend was important to him.

It was nice they'd grown so close in such a short time.

Still, Kate wasn't proud of the flare of resentment that slithered through her belly.

13

E than glanced at Kate seated beside him in the Lifeline chopper, trying to figure out what was going on behind those chameleon eyes of hers. She could've been on the far side of the moon for all the emotional distance she put between them.

Reese's voice crackled through his headset. "Lifeline to base, we're running into scattered patches of fog. Visibility is still about ninety percent, so we are still on course to reach Cedar Bluff Hospital in fifteen minutes."

"Ten-four."

They'd received the flight call first thing that morning, which meant he hadn't had time to ask Kate how her grandfather was feeling. Three days had passed since he'd driven her home the night after her grandfather's open heart procedure. He'd offered to keep her company that night, to sleep on the sofa, but she'd refused.

And now, three days later, she still wouldn't look him in the eye.

Something was wrong, he wasn't so stupid he couldn't figure out at least that much. More was bothering Kate than just her grandfather's emergency heart surgery. And logic dictated that her avoidance of him was related to his confessing he was falling in love with her.

Guilt assailed him. Why had he blurted out the truth like that? Obviously, he'd frightened her. He wasn't sure why, but there was no denying something had changed between them. From the moment he'd seen her bouncing on the Hippity Hop, spraying Silly String at his daughter, he'd fallen for her. Hard.

Logically, he understood they hadn't known each other long, barely a couple of weeks. Yet he was old enough to know what he wanted in a woman and in a relationship, and he couldn't imagine his life without Kate.

Unfortunately, it was clear she didn't feel the same way.

A cement ball of doubt settled in Ethan's gut. Had he ruined things with Kate by rushing her? They'd only had the one date, but that didn't stop him from telling her how he felt. Why couldn't he have just followed his brain that had warned him to take things slow? Waited just a little longer?

"ETA three minutes."

Ethan glanced at Kate. Her attention was intensely focused on the flight report on her clipboard, which only had a few of the lines filled in. Once they landed at Cedar Bluff Hospital to pick up their patient, every line would be completed. He'd already gotten a brief report from the physician on duty. Their patient was a young man, twenty-three years old, with severe pulmonary hypertension. Rick Roberts had been recently placed on the lung transplant list and as a result needed immediate transport to Trinity.

Reese landed the chopper. He jumped out, Kate right behind him. Together they rounded the helicopter to remove the gurney from the back. He gestured for her to step away so he could pull the gurney out himself; there was no reason to stress her sore shoulder. But she ignored him, taking hold of the opposite end of the gurney and lifting it out with him.

Stubborn woman. Ethan pushed the stretcher away from the helipad toward the hospital's emergency room entrance. Inside, he took off his helmet, noticing Kate did the same.

"How's your shoulder?" He glanced at her as they made their way to the elevator and the ICU.

"Fine. It's better every day."

"You never did see the orthopod, did you?"

"Not yet." She shrugged "I did make an appointment, though, I believe it's next week. Trust me, I'd like to get off this lifting restriction as much as you would like me to."

He ground his teeth in frustration. She'd misunderstood him again. He cared more about her shoulder and preventing further injury than he did about whether or not he had to take over most of the lifting. Before he could comment and clear the air, they'd reached the ICU.

"Ginny, the Lifeline crew is here," someone called when they entered.

A cute, redheaded nurse hurried over. "Hi there. Rick Roberts is all ready to go."

Ethan smiled, though his attention was centered on Kate, whose somber attitude hadn't improved during the ride in. It was so unlike her. Where was her laughter? Her jokes? He really missed her smile. "Great. Is there a physician here who can update me on Mr. Robert's condition?"

"No, I'm sorry he's not available. I can tell you the patient has been stable." Ginny gestured to the bedside. "Come on, I'll introduce you."

The three of them entered the room.

"Rick, this is Dr. Weber and flight nurse Kate Lawrence. They are here to transport you to Trinity Medical Center so you can get your lung transplant."

"Hi." Rick's voice was faint. Ethan figured the guy was lucky not to be on a ventilator, although the best treatment for pulmonary hypertension was to keep the patient off the breathing machine for as long as possible. Once placed on a ventilator, a patient's lung disease tended to deteriorate rapidly. "Wow. Guess I'm traveling in style."

"Yep, you sure are." Kate grinned. Ethan was amazed at the transformation, and his chest ached because she hadn't smiled like that for him. At least not since their one and only date. "Lifeline limousine at your service." She gave Rick a mock bow and patted the empty gurney. "Your chariot awaits."

"I feel like a fraud," Rick said as they helped him move over from the bed to the gurney. The young man was very weak, so Ethan made sure to do most of the heavy lifting. "Shouldn't you be using the helicopter for people who really need it?"

"Hey, why should the trauma patients have all the fun?" Kate quickly switched over the cables to their portable equipment. "You know, once in a while it's nice to transport a patient who can appreciate our luxurious accommodations."

Ethan strapped him on the gurney, and Rick gave a weak smile. "Luxurious. Yeah. Right."

"Besides, you are on some pretty high doses of medication that require close monitoring," Ethan added. He knew looks could be deceptive. Rick seemed to be doing very well, but actually, he was breathing heavily from the small act of transferring onto the gurney. Ethan took note of how the patient's heart rate had also increased dramatically while the oxygen level in his blood had dropped by several points.

Rick hadn't been intubated and placed on a ventilator yet, but in all honesty, Ethan suspected if he didn't get a lung transplant soon, the young man would die.

The realization was sobering.

"Ready to roll?" Kate patted Rick's arm. "You're the boss on this flight. Customer service is our specialty. We aim to please."

Ethan couldn't help but smile as Kate continued her lighthearted routine. She kept calling Rick sir as if they were really boarding some exclusive chartered flight.

They wheeled Rick out to the waiting helicopter. Reese came out to quickly assist with lifting the patient through the hatch, then once they were all settled inside, prepared for the return flight.

Kate placed the headphones over Rick's ears so she could continue to chat with him. "Hmmm. We seem to be all out of coffee, tea, and soda. How about a little normal saline instead?" She grinned as she connected a new IV bag to his nearly empty line.

Ethan lost his balance as Reese banked the chopper, and he shook his head, feeling as if he'd entered a time warp. Kate's sunny face suddenly reminded him of the very first time they'd met, when he'd been so preoccupied with Carly and his childcare problems. He'd assumed she'd been coming on to him. But now he knew that was mostly because deep down he'd been fighting a strong attraction to her.

But what about the men in her life before him? She claimed she had a few male friends, but now he thought that might not be the case at all. The more he thought about it, the harder it was for him to believe it. Kate was beautiful, inside and out, with a great, if quirky, sense of humor. Her strong family loyalty was also endearing. It was possible each of her relationships had started out the same way his had, with Kate's lighthearted fun approach. Was it possible the other men she'd seen had wanted more but she'd shut them down?

He was beginning to think this on the surface type of relationship had been her specialty, until she crossed the line with him. They'd hugged and kissed and grown close. But now it was obvious she was backing off. Somehow, he didn't think her sudden need for distance was because she didn't like his kiss but simply because of his declaration of falling in love.

Could it be that he'd given his heart to a woman who didn't want a serious relationship? His hope sank as he considered the painful truth. Especially, perhaps, because a relationship with him came with a ready-made family.

KATE WAS TRYING her best to focus on Rick, but Ethan's magnetic presence overwhelmed the cramped interior of the helicopter to the exclusion of everything else.

She couldn't even explain why she'd been trying to avoid him. At first, fear and worry over Granddad had kept her from thinking about how Ethan had professed his love. But last night she hadn't been able to sleep, replaying that moment over and over in her mind.

How was it possible that his kisses had changed her? Each and every one of her nerve endings seemed to be in tune with him, distracting her with the urge to touch him.

This obsession of hers had to stop. Ethan had a daughter, and even if he did think he was in love with her, she knew he probably only said the words out of wanting a mother for his daughter not true love. Whatever feelings he had for her would soon fade, and he'd move on to someone else. They always did. She had no reason to think Ethan would be any different.

"Kate? I don't feel so good." Rick's quiet voice was barely above a whisper.

Her gaze instantly sought the heart monitor, verifying that his vital signs were stable. "What's wrong, Rick? You feel sick to your stomach? Or light-headed and dizzy?"

"Let's verify his medication infusion," Ethan suggested, pulling out his phone calculator app. "Let's make sure we didn't miscalculate the infusion rate."

"Sick to my stomach," Rick confided. He managed a weak smile. "Maybe I'm airsick."

"Well, that's impossible because we don't allow air sickness to bother our patients while they are enjoying Lifeline's limousine service," she teased. "There must be something else going on here."

"His IVs are all running at the correct rates," Ethan informed her. "Give him five milligrams of Compazine."

"All right." Taking medication out of the bag, she dropped the dose and injected it into Rick's normal saline IV line. "This medication is for nausea," she told him. "Hopefully, you'll feel better soon."

"Thanks." Rick closed his eyes, his face pale and drawn. Her heart squeezed painfully in her chest. He was only twenty-three years old and facing possible death if he didn't get a lung transplant. And even then, how long would he have to live? Another ten to fifteen years? Antirejection meds made every transplant patient more susceptible to illnesses, so anything longer than that was highly unlikely.

The thought made her sad.

"Reese, how long until we reach Trinity?" Ethan asked.

"ETA eighteen minutes," Reese responded.

Kate trusted Ethan, but she also glanced at the medication bags, making sure everything was running correctly. Some of this medication was powerful stuff. One minor miscalculation could have harsh consequences. She traced the IV tubing back to the catheter, twisting the connecting ports to make sure they weren't loose.

"Ethan, take a look at this." Kate tugged Rick's hospital gown out of the way to show him the central line site. "I think it's leaking at the site."

Ethan's solemn gaze met hers. "You're right—good catch. I'll try to start another line on the other side."

They worked together. Kate handed Ethan supplies before he asked for them, trying to reassure Rick as Ethan slid another catheter into a vein in the side of his neck. Ethan was good, he hit the vein on the first try, and Kate transferred the medication infusion from the leaky catheter to the new one.

She took her time flushing the old line, not wanting to bolus Rick with whatever medication was left over in the catheter.

Reese landed at Trinity Medical Center's heliport a short while later. She stayed with Rick as Ethan went out to withdraw him out from the back, then jumped down after him.

Once inside the ICU, Rick was feeling better, and they were able to transfer his care without difficulty. Rick clutched her hand tight when she bent over him to say goodbye.

"Take care of yourself, Rick. I'll come back and visit after you get your transplant," she promised.

"Good. I'd like that." His voice was weak, but his smile was all heart.

On the way out to the chopper, Ethan glanced at her. "I didn't get a chance to ask this morning, but how is your grandfather doing?"

"Oh, he's doing great. He was transferred out of the ICU yesterday. I'm heading over to visit him after work tonight." Kate didn't add how her granddad didn't seem to need her much now that Miranda was with him. Her disgruntled feelings were petty, but she couldn't seem to get a grip. Granddad was obviously happy. And honestly, she'd secretly investigated Miranda only to find the woman was as nice as she seemed to be, not the gold-digger she'd originally thought. Kate knew she should be doing cartwheels to see her granddad doing so well.

So why wasn't she?

"I can go with you, if you'd like," Ethan offered.

"Oh, thanks, but I'm fine. I know you have to get home for Carly." Kate ducked her head and jabbed the elevator button. She was being an idiot, but she couldn't seem to help herself. It would be better to break away from Ethan now rather than wait until later.

But she hadn't anticipated just how much she would miss him. A part of her wanted to pull him close, the other part of her wanted to run as fast and as far as she could.

"Kate, Carly is doing much better. She hasn't tormented the nanny in almost three days." He paused and cleared his throat. "I'd like to come with you."

Panicked, she glanced at him. Why was he doing this? Didn't he know how difficult it was for her to be with him? But what could she say? No? "I guess that's fine."

He frowned at her less than enthusiastic response, and she stared at the elevator floor, praying they reached the rooftop helipad quickly. The silence hung thick and heavy like wet snow between them.

Once on board the chopper, they didn't have time to talk because another call came in—this time a scene call from a multiple motor vehicle crash.

It was a bad one. Black smoke billowed out of a pile of burning cars. Although they landed nearby and hauled out their gear, rushing over to offer aid, Kate was fairly certain there wouldn't be many survivors

The semitruck had crossed the center line and crashed head-on into several other cars in the oncoming lane of traffic. Kate and Ethan helped as much as they could at the scene, but each person they pulled from the record wreckage was beyond hope.

By the time they'd finished, seven people were dead, including the truck driver.

Not a single survivor.

The ride back to Lifeline was especially quiet. Ethan's flight suit, as well as hers, smelled of smoke and was stained with blood. Once they reached the hangar, they both changed into fresh flight suits and tossed theirs into the washing machine that was kept in the hangar just for this purpose.

They spent so much time at the crash scene their shift was nearly over. Still deeply bothered by the needless loss of life, Kate busied herself with paperwork as a way to avoid another conversation with Ethan. By the time the oncoming shift arrived, she was more than ready to go.

Without waiting for Ethan, she ducked out of the debriefing room and headed outside. She drove her car around the Lifeline hangar to Trinity's parking structure.

Inside the hospital, she walked to Granddad's room. He was on the third floor, just down the hall from the CICU. Straightening her shoulders and pasting a bright smile on her face, she knocked on his door before peeking in.

"Granddad? It's Kate." She pushed the door open and wasn't surprised to see Miranda seated in a chair at Granddad's bedside, holding his hand.

Miranda had been there day all day and well into the evening, ever since Kate had first called her with the news. The woman was sure taking her role as Granddad's girlfriend seriously.

"Hello, Kate." Miranda beamed. "Tony has been waiting for you."

"Sorry, but our shift ended a little late." Kate crossed over and bent to give him a quick kiss on the cheek. "You look great. Have you been up walking today?"

"Of course, I have. Do you think the nurses here would allow me to slack off? Not a chance. They're evil taskmasters."

She was relieved to see that his color was good and his voice was almost back to normal.

"Great. I guess the bribe money is working."

Granddad laughed as she'd hoped he would.

"Sit down, Kate. I have some wonderful news to tell you." Granddad gestured to the second chair in the room.

"Really? What's that—you won the lottery?" Kate dropped into the only empty chair, although she felt awkward sitting across from the cozy couple.

"No, something far better." Granddad lifted Miranda's hand and kissed it. "Miranda has agreed to be my wife. We are getting married."

14

Her smile froze, and she suspected her face resembled that of a ridiculous cartoon character. There was a long pause before she could make her jaw work enough to speak. "Congratulations. I'm happy for you."

Kate knew her granddad wasn't fooled when he frowned. "Katie girl, I don't know what's wrong with you lately. You having boyfriend trouble?"

"No, of course not." Kate didn't even want to think of how she'd sneaked away from Ethan just ten minutes earlier. Yeah, she was having boyfriend problems all right.

The man thought he loved her when she knew very well that he didn't.

"Humph. I don't believe you." Granddad glared at her. "When are you gonna stop running away from love?"

"I'm not," she protested, sitting straighter in the chair.

"Yes, you are. I recognize the signs. I did the same thing for years, you know. But now . . ." He looked over at Miranda, and his expression softened. "I know exactly what I was missing. And I refuse to let a second chance go to waste." He sighed and turned back to Kate. "We're getting married on Saturday right here in the hospital chapel."

"What? Saturday? Are you crazy? You can't. Granddad, that's only two days away. Mom and Dad are still in Europe. Why can't you wait another ten days until they come back?"

"Because I don't want to. Saturday is the day I'm scheduled to be discharged, if all goes as planned, and I don't want to waste another moment." Granddad nodded as if he hadn't dropped a bomb. "Katie girl, it's time for you to stop avoiding the truth. Skating along the surface of one relationship to another isn't healthy. Trust me, I know what I'm talking about."

"I agree, Mr. Lawrence."

Kate snapped her head around in shock when Ethan entered the room. "What are you doing here?" She sounded ridiculously like a petulant child, and she knew it.

"I came here to be with you, remember? But you left without me." He crossed the room, extending his head to Granddad. "I'm Ethan Weber, a friend of Kate's. It's nice to meet you."

"Heh, heh, heh." Granddad had the audacity to chuckle as he shook Ethan's hand. "Well, now, it's nice to meet you, too. So, you're a friend of Kate's, are you? The one she cooked for?"

"That's right." Ethan rocked back on his heels. "How did you know? Oh, I see, you must've helped her plan the meal. It was great, by the way."

"I did," her granddad agreed. "And I must say I'm glad everything was a roaring success."

They were talking over her as if she didn't exist, and she was growing seriously annoyed. Although she also felt wobbly, as if she'd just donated a pint of blood, instead of hearing Granddad's plan to marry Miranda. Not just marry her but to have the ceremony here in the hospital in two days. She forced herself to stand. "Look, I have to head home. I'm glad you're doing so well, Granddad."

"Wait, you can't leave yet." Granddad raised his hand as if to stop her. "Miranda wants to know if you'll stand up with her at our wedding."

Stand up? Like a bridesmaid? Seriously? Kate glanced back and saw the hopeful expression on Miranda's gently lined face and felt like a complete heel. "Of course. I'm honored. What about a dress? Is there something specific you'd like me to wear?"

"Oh, anything nice is fine with me." Miranda smiled and squeezed Granddad's hand. "I'm wearing an ivory dress, so you can choose any color in any length you like that might match. Doesn't have to be something new either." She smiled at Granddad, then turned back toward Kate. "I'm thrilled you'll be my maid of honor."

"Me, too. It will be great. Well, then." Kate subtly edged closer to the door. "Now I really have to go so I can scour the contents of my closet. If I can't find something nice to wear, I'll head to the store. Congrats again, Miranda, Granddad." She ducked through the doorway, heading blindly into the hall.

"Omphf." She bumped into someone and took a faltering step back. A man's large hands came up to grasp her shoulders long enough to steady her.

"Kate?" a male voice said in surprise. "Wow, it's nice to see you. How are you?"

"Klutzy, apparently. Sorry about that. How are you, Daniel? Is cardiology keeping you busy?" She recognized the tall, slender cardiology resident, Daniel Jones, a guy she'd had some fun with last year. He'd gone through a rough time when one of his fellow residents had passed away unexpectedly, and she'd helped him get over the loss.

"Yeah, pretty much." He tilted his head, regarding her thoughtfully. His voice dropped in pitch. "You look great, Kate."

"Thanks. So do you." She forced herself to stand calmly when all she really wanted to do was run home. Her day was going from bad to worse. She noticed Daniel's gaze set on something over her shoulder, and at the same time, she felt Ethan step up behind her. Ethan placed a possessive hand on her arm.

"Are you busy? Oh, er, never mind." Daniel grinned ruefully at Ethan. "I can see the two of you are together." He lifted a hand. "See you around, Kate." He nodded at Ethan, and added, "Good luck."

"Thanks, I have a feeling I'll need it," was Ethan's dry reply.

What was that about? Kate frowned and shrugged off Ethan's grip. "I have to go and so do you. Carly's waiting, I'm sure."

"We need to talk." Ethan's voice was grim.

"About what?" She crossed her arms defensively over her chest.

He sighed. "Who was that guy? Someone you dated?"

"Yes, he's a friend, we went out for a few weeks when he was having some trouble. I helped him find his sense of humor." Kate couldn't figure out what Ethan was getting at. "So?"

"So, he was looking at you as if he wanted far more than simple friendship. Like you were a tasty meal and he hadn't eaten in weeks." Ethan shoved his hands into his pockets. "I thought the men in your life didn't want a relationship with you?"

"He didn't," she protested, but doubt had already begun to creep in. Daniel had looked at her strangely until Ethan had shown up. She thought he'd simply been surprised to see her. But maybe . . .

"You know, I think your grandfather is right. You are running, Kate. The minute our relationship turned personal, turned real, you backed off."

"Are you finished psychoanalyzing me yet? Because I need to find a dress."

"Your grandfather's wedding is really bothering you," Ethan observed. "Probably because of your own fear of commitment."

"I'm not upset," she lied, desperately wishing she could leave. "You don't know what you're talking about. I have to go."

She brushed past, desperate to get away.

"Kate?" His voice stopped her midstride. Hesitating, she turned back to look at him. "I'll let you go if that's what you really want. But if you ever get sick of running, give me a call."

Irrationally, her heart squeezed painfully. Did he really mean to cut off their friendship? Just like that?

Hiding her wounded soul, she shrugged. "I'll see you at work, Ethan." Before he could continue to tell her what else was wrong with her, she made a quick escape.

At home, she told herself Ethan didn't know what he was talking about. Rummaging through her closet, she pulled out and tried several dresses, discarding each of them for one reason or another. She wasn't running from anything. Was it her fault Miranda wanted her to stand up for the wedding? Having the proper dress was important, and it wasn't like she had time to waste.

After what seemed like hours, with the contents of her

entire closet strewn about the room, she finally settled on a satin dress in a pretty forest green. Hopefully, Miranda would like it, she thought grimly as she began the tedious task of cleaning up.

Would Ethan see her in it? Doubtful.

Later that night, she stared blankly at the ceiling, unable to sleep. The familiar heavy weight of depression and hopelessness settled over her heart, just like in the days following David's death.

For years she'd emulated her grandfather's relationships, seeing her job as wanting to spread fun and laughter to those who needed it most. Ethan had been a prime example of someone who needed her help. The man hadn't smiled until she'd shown him how to have fun.

Now, though, she forced herself to face the truth. Keeping things light without allowing for anything more was a form of running. She had pushed Ethan away when he'd gotten so serious. David's death had taught her how much love hurt. Holding men at arm's length was her subconscious way to avoid getting hurt like that again.

Which was exactly what had happened. Thinking about life without Ethan and Carly hurt far worse than anything she felt after those dark days on the heels of David's suicide. Precious Carly, with her wide, too adult eyes, thrilled with her very own dream catcher. Ethan's solid strength in helping her resuscitate Granddad, then coming back to the hospital, after making arrangements for Carly, just to be there for her.

Her chest ached, and her stomach clenched painfully.

All this time she thought she was helping them when, in reality, they had shown her something new, too. Ethan and Carly had given her a glimpse of what life could be like with a family of her own.

Except she'd blown her chance. Ethan hadn't left her the way David had. No, this time, as with all the other relationships in her life, she'd been the one to walk away.

The pain was hot and sharp, but there was no one to blame but herself.

KATE DROVE like a madman into work, breaking every speed limit in the book. She'd overslept and could only imagine how annoyed the night shift was going to be with her tardiness.

She'd awoken with a new sense of purpose. Okay, so maybe love had hurt her once. But it didn't have to hurt forever. Hadn't Ethan told her to call if she decided to stop running? Well, she would.

Soon.

Today.

With her foot on the brake, she squealed around a tight curve, then raced into the Lifeline parking lot. She parked her car haphazardly, then ran inside.

Was Ethan working too? She thought they were scheduled together when she entered the debriefing room, though, disappointment stabbed deep.

Zane Taylor was the physician seated in the chair waiting for her instead of Ethan. There was no sign of the night crew. They'd obviously debriefed without her.

"Sorry I'm late," she apologized quickly. "Anything new?"

Zane shook his head. "You didn't miss much. Is your grandfather doing all right? You don't look as if you got very much sleep."

"He's fine, should be discharged tomorrow." Kate

avoided the topic of Granddad's wedding. "Do we have a call?"

"No, the chopper is down for maintenance." Zane flashed an evil grin at her crestfallen expression. "If you had called to say you were running late, I would've told you not to hurry."

"I can't believe it," she groaned, dropping into a nearby chair. "All that rushing around for nothing."

"Yep." Zane's tone was positively cheerful. "Guess you'll get to do follow-up visits today."

The idea of doing post-flight follow-up visits brightened her mood. She liked seeing how their Lifeline patients fared after their transfer. Still, it was a little early for visits. She glanced at the schedule. And frowned. "Why did you switch shifts with Ethan?" She tried to keep her tone nonchalant even though she was dying to know.

"He called, saying he needed the next two days off." Zane lifted the shoulder. "I didn't ask why. He's working for me Sunday and Monday instead."

"I see." Kate swallowed hard, accepting the truth that Ethan was avoiding her. She couldn't really blame him but was disappointed all the same. A sense of urgency had her tapping her fingers on the clipboard. How early could she call Ethan, anyway? Carly must need to get up for school. Should she wait until after Carly had left for the day?

She bit her lip with uncertainty. What if he'd changed his mind? What if he hadn't meant what he'd said about falling in love with her? What if—

Stop it! Kate put her hands over her ears in an effort to silence the doubting voice in her head. All she needed to do was get through her shift, then she could talk to Ethan. Tell him what a fool she'd been and how sorry she was for being stupid.

Surely, he'd give her a second chance.

Kate couldn't believe how slowly the day dragged by. She finished her follow-up visits in record time, seeing all the patients they recently transported. The young college student with the eight, yes, eight chest tubes had undergone surgery and now only had two chest tubes. He was doing much better and had been transferred out of the ICU. The biker dude was doing fairly well, although still confused from his head injury. Even the Miranda look-alike patient, Lucille, was doing well. The only patient she hadn't been able to see was Rick Roberts, the lung transplant patient, because he was in surgery, getting a new set of lungs. Hopefully, he'd do well after his transplant, and she made a notation to do another follow-up visit on him in a few days.

Unable to stand it a moment longer, she picked up the phone and quickly dialed Ethan's number. When he didn't answer, she waited another hour and called again. And again. By the fourth time, she knew his number by heart. Each time, the phone rang three times before his deep husky voice sounded on the recording. "Hi, I'm busy but leave your name and number and I'll call you back."

Just listening to his voice made her want to see him. She'd hung up the last three times she called, but her shift was almost over. Gathering her courage, she left him a message.

"Ethan, it's Kate. You told me to call, so I'm calling." Brilliant, just brilliant. She inwardly groaned. "If you're not doing anything tomorrow, I'll be at Granddad's wedding." She paused, then added, "I'd like to talk."

She slowly disconnected from the call. Maybe he'd return her call yet tonight. Kate sat in the debriefing for the next shift, then headed home.

She pulled out everything she needed for her granddad's

wedding, laying out her dress, shoes, and handbag in an orderly fashion. She tried to eat, although she wasn't hungry. Finally, she went to bed.

Ethan didn't return her call.

Trinity Medical Center staff were thrilled to have a wedding of a former patient in their chapel. Granddad was officially a former patient because he'd been discharged first thing that morning.

A small group of people gathered in the chapel, waiting for the minister to arrive. Kate had tried once again to convince Granddad to wait for her parents to come home from their trip, but he refused to consider even a short delay. He claimed he was too old to care about what his son and daughter-in-law thought. As long as Kate was there, that was all he needed.

She smoothed a sweaty hand down the side of her dress. Inside, she was agonizing over her stupidity in pushing Ethan away, but today was Granddad's special day, and she was not going to ruin it for him.

She felt as if she'd ruined enough already.

"Miranda, you look beautiful." Kate clasped the older woman's cold, frail hands in hers and gave her a warm smile. "Granddad is a very lucky man."

"Oh, Kate." Miranda blushed and squeezed her hands. "Thank you, but I'm the fortunate one. Finding him again after all these years, well, I just have to believe this was meant to be."

"Again?" Kate wrinkled her brow. "You knew him before? When?"

"Yes, he and I first met in college. He, well, he was my first love."

Kate was surprised at the news. "But you broke up,

married other people, then fell in love again all these years later?" The idea was mind-boggling.

"Tony has always held a special place in my heart, but yes, we both went our separate ways. We married, had families, and now we're both widowers, you know," she confided as if it were a big secret. "It just seems right to be with him again after all these years."

"Well, I'm very happy for both of you." True sincerity rang through Kate's tone because she meant every word. "Honestly, I haven't ever seen Granddad so happy."

"Thank you." Miranda spotted the minister. "Oh, I think we're finally ready to get started." She hurried off.

Kate saw a familiar towheaded girl clutching the hand of a handsome dark-haired man who stood beside her granddad. For a moment, her heart soared. Ethan had come! Then, just as quickly, it plummeted to her feet. The expression on his face as he talked to Granddad told her he'd been there for a few minutes.

Ethan hadn't come for her. He'd come for Granddad. Even Carly didn't run over to talk to her but stood admiring Miranda's ivory lace dress.

Kate blinked rapidly, staving off tears. *Don't cry, this is Granddad's day. Don't cry!*

The minister quickly took charge, shifting everyone around the room. He positioned Kate on one side of the altar, and Kate was surprised to see Ethan standing next to Granddad on the opposite side. She glanced at him inquiringly, but he simply smiled and nodded at her, then focused his attention on Miranda when the music began to play.

Music from Bach's *Fantasy in G Major* filled the chapel. Kate smiled as Miranda slowly walked up the short aisle to Granddad. He stood, leaning heavily on his cane as she took his arm. He beamed, then proudly turned and faced the minister.

"We are gathered here today to celebrate the marriage of Anthony Lawrence and Miranda Purdy . . ."

The service was sweetly romantic and over all too soon. There was a wheelchair nearby for Granddad as he still had a long way to go before being back to his old self. Kate was surprised to see him sink into the chair, allowing Miranda to push him through the room.

Kate tried to find a good time to duck out. So far she'd managed to avoid conversing with Ethan, but the chapel wasn't that big, and there weren't very many people, so her stall tactic would work for long.

"Kate!" Carly ran toward her, throwing her arms around her waist in a big hug. "You are so beautiful. Green is my favorite color! I missed you."

Tears threatened again, clogging her throat so she could barely speak. "I've missed you, too, Carly."

"You wanted to talk?" Ethan's deep voice drew her gaze upward to where he stood behind his daughter.

"Hello, Ethan. It was nice of you to stand up with Granddad."

"My pleasure." He glanced toward the newlyweds. "He's a great guy."

Her eyes misted at the admiration in his tone. "I know."

"Kate." Ethan reached out to grasp her hand. "I'm sorry we weren't home yesterday. Carly's friend came down with the chicken pox, and I had to find the pediatrician records to confirm she'd had her booster before they let her go back to school. Then she ate something that made her sick—"

"I throwed up," Carly added helpfully.

"It's all right, I understand," she interrupted. "Really."

"You do?" His tone was wary as if he knew there was something he was missing.

"I don't have the chicken pox," Carly announced. "See?" She held out her arms. "No pox."

Kate had to laugh. "I'm glad." For the first time, she realized Ethan might not have changed his mind after all. She glanced at Granddad who caught her gaze and winked.

Suddenly, she knew just what to do. Capturing Carly's hand, she knelt in front of the child. "Carly, I have a very important question to ask you."

The girl tilted her head to the side. "What's that?"

"I want to know if you'll give me permission to ask your Dad to marry me."

Carly's eyes widened in surprise. "Isn't he supposed to ask you?"

Kate's knees were knocking from nervousness, but she shook her head. "Not necessarily."

"Yes, he is." Ethan raised his voice over hers, reaching out and drawing her to her feet. He tucked her close, his arm strong around her. "Kate, will you marry me? Be a family with us?" With his other hand, he brought Carly into their embrace.

"Yes. I will." Kate wrapped her arms around both of them. "I love you, Ethan."

"It's about time," he muttered before capturing her mouth in a deep kiss.

Carly squirmed away and ran toward Granddad and Miranda. "Great-Grandpa, guess what? My dad's gonna marry Kate, and I don't have the chicken pox, see?"

Ethan lifted his mouth from hers and grinned. "Are you sure you know what you're in for?" His tone was full of doubt. "Things have moved pretty fast. Maybe we should slow it down, give you some time to adjust."

"I don't need to slow down." Kate didn't have a single doubt. Not anymore. Not about him. She leaned on Ethan and knew she was home at last. "I'm through with running. I love you, and I love Carly." Her voice dropped to a mere whisper. "My new family."

DEAR READER

I hope you're enjoying my *Lifeline Air Rescue Series* built off my personal ride along in our very own Flight For Life. The theme of this story is laughter, and I am a firm believer, like Kate, in the power of positive thinking and in laughter being the best medicine.

Reviews are critically important to authors, so if you enjoyed this book, please consider putting up a review on the platform where you purchased it from. I would appreciate it very much!

I love hearing from my readers and can be contacted via my website at www.laurascottbooks.com, through Facebook at Laura Scott Author, and on Twitter @laurascottbooks. Also, if you haven't signed up for my newsletter, please do. I offer a free Crystal Lake novella for all newsletter subscribers.

If you are curious about the next book in my Lifeline Air Rescue Series, the first chapter of *A Doctor's Trust* is included for your reading pleasure.

Until next time,

Laura Scott

A DOCTOR'S TRUST

Her seventeen-year-old sister was late. Again.

Jenna Reed opened one eye and looked at the illuminated tiles of her clock. Yup, almost midnight. Rae's curfew was 2330. Where in the world was she?

Exhaling a long breath, Jenna flopped onto her back and untwisted her ratty T-shirt from the sheet. Outside, ribald shouts coalesced with the heavy beat of rap music. Not that the noise was unusual for a Thursday night—this area, dubbed Barclay Park, located in the heart of Milwaukee, was rarely quiet. Her house was packed like a sardine beside her neighbors', and the walls were paper thin. She used to sleep like a rock.

Unless her sister happened to be out with Nelson, her numskull boyfriend. Then sleep was next to impossible. Rae didn't care if Jenna had to be up at 0600 to make it to work at Lifeline Air Rescue by seven.

Or maybe her sly sister was actually banking on that fact, hoping to sneak in without waking her.

Ha! Fat chance.

Squealing tires and a thunderous crash jolted her from bed.

"Help! Someone help!"

Jenna rushed outside, sparing no more than two seconds to jam her feet into the flip-flop sandals lying beside the door. Her eyes widened when she saw what all the fuss was about. A car had smashed headfirst into the light pole not far from the abandoned lot across the street. Instantly, her paramedic training kicked in.

She hurried to the crash site, pushing her way through the small crowd. "How many people are inside?" Jenna peered through the windows. "Two?"

"Three. Two adults in front and baby in the backseat," one teen pointed out.

"Anyone hurt?" She tried to open the driver's door, but it was seriously dented and wouldn't budge. Through the window, she could see the driver was slumped over, his face covered in blood. The airbag had deployed, but his face had still been cut from the force of the blow.

"Call nine-one-one, tell them we have two adults and one infant involved in a single-car crash, and the driver is seriously injured," she directed.

A familiar pierced, purple-haired teenager, about the same age as her sister, used her cell phone for something more useful than text messaging. She didn't pay attention to the nine-one-one call, working instead on finding a way into the car. All the doors were locked, so she made her way around to the passenger side where the back window happened to be opened a few inches.

"They're sending the Lifeline helicopter," the breathless purple-haired teen informed her.

"They are?" Jenna lifted a brow in surprise. Normally, they didn't send the chopper into the city unless the crew just happened to be close by. Especially since there weren't always available spots to land.

"How are we gonna get them out?" The teen—what was her name? Luanne?—peered anxiously inside the car.

"Very carefully." Jenna stepped around the broken glass from the windshield shattered by the airbag deployment. Sneaking her arm through the tiny opening, she reached down. It wasn't easy, but she managed to hit the unlock button with the tip of her finger.

"There." With the back doors unlocked, they could at least get to the wailing infant. Thank heavens the kid was protected in a car seat.

There wasn't time for Jenna to run back inside the house for her stethoscope. She could tell the difference between seriously injured and stable without the aid of medical equipment. In examining the baby, there wasn't a speck of blood to be seen. He looked fine, with a healthy set of lungs.

"Here, keep an eye on him for me." She handed the crying infant to Luanne, who was standing with a group of other kids Jenna recognized from MCCT, the Milwaukee Community Center for Teens program. Apparently, Rae wasn't the only one out late.

Back inside the car, she crawled up between the seats. The woman in the passenger seat groaned, moving restlessly. Jenna zeroed in on the still, silent driver. She pressed two fingers along his neck, searching for a carotid pulse.

For a moment she feared the worst and then felt a slight, thready beat. Relief washed over her. He was still alive, although the distinctive scent of alcohol made her wrinkle her nose. "Hey, mister, can you hear me?"

No response. She stared at the driver's chest. He was breathing, but the motion was shallow. He'd need medical attention pretty quick. She glanced around the interior of the car. How could she get him out without causing potentially more damage?

She turned her attention to the passenger. "Ma'am? Can you hear me?"

"Yes." The voice was faint, and Jenna figured she was only slightly better off than the driver. The airbags had deployed, which was probably the only reason they were still alive.

"What hurts?"

"Everything, but mostly my chest." The woman grimaced, then asked, "Where's Matthew? My baby?"

"Matthew is fine. Not hurt a bit. Now don't move. Help will be here soon," Jenna reassured her. She took note that neither the driver nor the passenger had been wearing seat belts, despite the seat belt law in Wisconsin.

The whirling beat of the Lifeline chopper overhead, along with the distinctive wail of sirens, echoed through the night. She didn't dare move the driver without further assistance, so she backed out of the car and pried open the passenger door to gain better access to the woman. The helicopter landed in the vacant lot. Two people dressed in flight suits pulled a gurney from the back of the chopper and headed across the litter-strewn blacktop to meet them.

She recognized the taller of the two and inwardly groaned. Of all the crew members on staff, why did Zane Taylor have to be the flight doctor on duty tonight?

"Jenna?" His eyes widened with recognition, and she was surprised he remembered her name. He stared for a long moment at her bare legs, and she resisted the urge to tug at the hem of her T-shirt. She was wearing shorts but still felt completely underdressed. "You live around here?" His tone was laced with incredulous concern.

Hoping the darkness hid her scarlet cheeks, she chose to

ignore his question. "We have a young woman with a blunt chest trauma, complaining of chest pain." Concentrating on work helped to cover up her mortification. "The driver is also suffering blunt trauma, including an apparent head injury. The airbags did deploy, but neither were wearing their seat belts. The driver is in bad shape, has alcohol on board, and is not responding to verbal commands. He did have a pulse, but the rate is fast and his breathing shallow."

"Let's take a look." Zane oozed confidence she envied.

Overly conscious of how she must look in her threadbare sleep shirt, without a bra or shoes, Jenna would've given her entire life savings, earmarked for Rae's college, to slither away through the gathering crowd.

Kate, the flight nurse on duty, knelt beside the passenger, examining her. Zane went straight for the driver.

"Jenna, give me hand with this guy." Zane gestured for her to come over to the other side of the car.

Her chance to escape vanished.

Between them, she and Zane helped to get the driver out of his seat, protecting his spine as much as possible in case there were fractures they weren't aware of. Once they'd gotten him supine, they could begin taking care of him.

"Let's put a C-collar on him, then get him on the gurney so we can get him transported to the chopper."

Jenna pulled equipment out of the flight bag as he spoke, anticipating what they'd need. Her long straight unbound dark hair was a nuisance, and she shoved it aside with the back of her forearm to keep the strands out of her way. Once they had the driver safely transferred onto the gurney, Zane continued to dictate orders.

"I need to place an IV. Set up a normal saline infusion."

Jenna had only worked for Lifeline for the past few months and could count on one hand the number of times she'd been paired to fly with Zane, and that had been mostly during her training when a third person had been around as a diversion. For whatever reason, their schedules always differed—either they were on different shifts or he was working on her off days and vice versa. The simple bit of fate had suited her just fine.

Until tonight's curveball.

Zane threaded the catheter into the driver's vein, then she took over, connecting the tubing and regulating his fluids. She already had him hooked up to the heart monitor, the beat was fast but sinus rhythm, a good sign. From there, it didn't take long to have him ready to go.

Strange, but working with Zane was easier than she'd anticipated, as if they'd been partners for years.

"Two liters of fluid have been infused, Dr. Taylor."

"Thanks." Zane flashed a quick, lethal smile. Her stomach clenched, and she fought the wave of awareness, knowing full well he smiled like that at everyone. It didn't mean a thing. Zane Taylor was so far out of her stratosphere she wasn't even on the same planet. He was as unreachable as Pluto while she was stuck on mere planet Earth.

Jenna took a hasty step back and winced at the sharp biting pain in her foot. Glancing down, she noticed her left foot was covered in blood. Whether it was hers or the driver's, she wasn't quite sure.

"What happened?" Zane must've noticed the direction of her gaze because he stared at her foot with concern while still clutching the edge of the gurney. "Sit down. We need to get one of the paramedics from the ambulance crew to take a look."

She forced a smile. "I am a paramedic, remember? Go on, take care of the trauma patient. I'm fine."

"Let them take a look." He sent her a no-nonsense glare,

then pushed the gurney toward the chopper. Kate had the female passenger on an ambulance gurney and gestured for the paramedics to take care of the infant and the mother. Within moments, Kate had joined Zane and they had stowed the driver in the back of the chopper, then went airborne. Soon the other paramedics prepared to leave as well.

She didn't bother asking one of them to look at her foot, they had better things to do. More important medical needs to address. She'd take care of it herself.

"Jenna?"

She turned and found Rae standing there, dressed in a tight miniskirt and a midriff-baring tank top. She hoped her sister and her goofy boyfriend weren't having unprotected sex. An unexpected pregnancy was the last thing she wanted to think about. Sex, drugs, and rap music were the norm in Barclay Park. Raising a teenager in this environment was far from easy.

"What happened here?" Rae gazed at the crash scene with morbid fascination.

"You're late," Jenna snapped. "Where have you been?"

Rae shrugged one bare shoulder. "Chill. We lost track of time. It's no big deal. Soon I have to start cramming for finals. Get off my back, *Sis.*" The sharp emphasis of the last word rankled. It was an old argument: Jenna was Rae's sister, not her mother.

But their mother was gone, and Jenna was all Rae had.

She stepped close and wrapped her arms around Rae in a big hug, a nice way of getting into her sister's face. No strong scent of alcohol or pot, thank heavens. That didn't rule out other drugs, but she preferred not to think the worst. Just two weeks until Rae graduated from high school, then another few months until she started college. Jenna's goal wouldn't be complete until Rae graduated from college, but finishing high school was proving to be the first hurdle.

Rae didn't tolerate the embrace for more than a split second. She broke away and rolled her eyes, then spun on her heel and stalked inside the house as if she always came home well after midnight on a school night.

Jenna sighed and followed more slowly, wincing with every painful step. Her own high school years were a blur. She couldn't remember going out to have fun, and sometimes it was hard not to resent Rae for her easy dismissal of the rules. Still, Jenna was grateful there was only one person dependent on her now.

With any luck, she'd pull herself out of debt soon.

As she doused her injured foot in the bathtub, looking for signs of embedded glass, Jenna tried not to remember Zane's reaction at finding her at the crash scene or the incredulous tone in his voice when he asked if she lived there.

She closed her eyes and leaned her overheated forehead against the cool tile. Good thing they didn't fly together often because she didn't think she could ever look him in the eye again. Now that he knew the truth, she planned to continue to avoid Zane Taylor in every way possible.

Jenna headed straight for the coffee when she entered Lifeline's lounge at ten minutes before 0700 hours.

"Good morning." Zane's voice startled her when she was about to take a sip, and she sloshed coffee down the front of her flight suit.

"Morning," she mumbled as she picked up a napkin and dabbed at the stain. Why was she such a klutz around him?

Taking a deep, fortifying breath, she tossed the napkin into the garbage, then turned toward him. Lifting her chin, she focused on a spot just behind his head. "So, how was the rest of your night?"

"Uneventful." To her chagrin, he stepped closer. The scent of his woodsy aftershave teased her senses. "How is your foot? Did you get the glass out?"

"It's fine," she lied. She hadn't found all the glass, and she could still feel a hidden shard with every step, but there was no way she was going to admit the truth. Besides, she'd learned in her training that foreign objects tended to work their way out of a wound eventually. After taking a careful sip of coffee, she glanced over his shoulder toward the debriefing room. "Guess we should go."

Zane didn't answer but walked behind her as they made their way across to the debriefing area. Walking normally had never been so difficult.

The day shift pilot, Reese Jarvis, was there, but there was still no sign of Jenna's crewmate. Jenna grabbed the schedule to see who was supposed to fly with her.

"Samantha needed the day off, so I'm covering the first four hours of her shift," Zane answered as if reading her mind. "After that, Dr. Kurt Simon will be in to work."

Jenna glanced at Reese in concern. "Is Sam all right?"

Dr. Samantha Jarvis was Reese's wife. He nodded, although his smile was feeble. "Yeah, but she scared the life out of me the way she was throwing up nonstop. Why is it called morning sickness if it doesn't happen only in the morning?" A frown furrowed his brow. "Shouldn't they just call it pregnancy sickness instead?"

Jenna lifted her shoulder in a helpless shrug. She was the last person to ask about birthing babies, unless you counted what she'd learned through her paramedic training. So far, she hadn't been forced to put her limited knowledge to use. "Sounds logical to me."

"Anyway, she's hoping to be back to work soon—if she can stop throwing up long enough to leave the house," Reese added. "I appreciate you covering for her, Taylor."

"No problem." Zane's drawl sent shivers of awareness zipping down her spine.

Distance. She needed distance. Then she remembered Zane was staying over for part of her shift. The news hadn't fully registered in her brain until that moment. So much for her plan to avoid him. Four hours. Not very long in the big scheme of things. She should be able to maintain a professional relationship for four hours.

Stealing her resolve, she glanced at Zane. "I was surprised to see the Lifeline chopper at the scene last night. How's the driver? Did you hear any news?"

"He's holding his own in the trauma ICU at Trinity Medical Center," Zane confirmed. "The female passenger was admitted to a cardiac step-down unit for observation, and she seems to be doing well, too. It just so happened we were on our way back from refueling and were close to the scene, so that's how we made it so fast. It was a good thing you were on hand to help."

She preferred not to remember the details of their bizarre meeting last night. "Any potential calls?"

"Yes, there was a call earlier this morning about a possible ICU transfer from Green Bay, but they were still waiting to get permission from the family. We are on standby for now."

"Sounds good." She turned toward Reese. "Any weather issues we need to know about?"

"Nope, clear skies and no wind. Should be a great day for flying."

Wonderful. Avoiding Zane wasn't an option, not if they were flying to Green Bay. Well, at least she didn't need to sit here and chat with him while they waited to hear about the transfer.

She stood and carried her empty coffee cup to the lounge. As she poured a refill, she heard someone come up behind her. Figuring it was Reese, she asked, "You don't normally drink coffee, do you? Being up all night with Samantha make you interested in trying it?"

"I love coffee, thanks." The deep timbre of Zane's voice caught her off guard. This time, though, she managed not to spill.

Swallowing hard, she poured a second cup and handed it to him. The slight touch of their fingertips sent a tingle through her hand, just like the last time she'd stuck a knife in the toaster to pry out a bagel. Stupid move on her part, yeah, but no worse than standing within touching distance of Zane Taylor.

"How long have you lived on Twenty-second Street in the Barclay Park area?" Zane asked. "It's not the greatest neighborhood."

She bristled, shooting him a narrow glare. Snob. He must be one of those people who took having money for granted. "Are you insinuating people don't drive drunk and hit light poles on the Hill?"

The Hill was a slang term for the Hills of Riverbend, a very nice suburban area located west of Milwaukee, where only the affluent could afford to live.

Where Zane Taylor lived.

Where she'd never in her entire life be able to live.

His eyebrows rose at her defensive tone. "I didn't say that. But now that you mention it, the Hill is a heck of a lot safer than Barclay Park. And I'm not worried about a drunk driving accident. We've gotten victims of multiple gunshot wounds from that area."

"There's nothing wrong with where I live." Jenna held on to her temper with an effort. Okay, he was right. Gunshots did occasionally ring out around them. But did Zane really think she chose to live in Barclay Park on purpose? Get real. No one in the right mind chose to live in one of the poorest sections of the city. But moneywise, it was the best she could afford.

All of which was none of his business.

She tried to sidestep him, intent on finding Reese. But her injured foot didn't cooperate. She couldn't hide a wince when the stabbing pain darted up toward her ankle. Ouch. She wouldn't last her entire twelve-hour shift if she didn't do something about the sliver of glass. The angle had been awkward, so she hadn't been able to see properly when she cleaned the area on her own.

"Sit down. Give me this." Zane lifted her coffee mug out of her hand with the grace she'd never have and set it aside without spilling a drop. Then he gently nudged her toward the sofa. "I'm examining your foot, and I'm not taking no for an answer."

www.ingramcontent.com/pod-product-compliance
Lightning Source LLC
Chambersburg PA
CBHW071804190726
48292CB00008B/2709